With Their
Best Clothes On

NEW WRITING SCOTLAND 36

Edited by
Susie Maguire
and
Samuel Tongue

Gaelic adviser
Rody Gorman

Association for Scottish Literary Studies

Association for Scottish Literary Studies
Scottish Literature, 7 University Gardens
University of Glasgow, Glasgow G12 8QH
www.asls.org.uk

ASLS is a registered charity no. SC006535

First published 2018

Images on pages 71, 73 and 75 © Steve J. McQueen, 2018.
Used by kind permission of the artist. Steve J. McQueen is a
Glasgow-based artist/maker and tutor. **stevejmcqueen.com**

British Library Cataloguing in Publication Data

A CIP record for this book is available
from the British Library

ISBN 978-1-906841-33-1

The Association for Scottish Literary Studies
acknowledges the support of Creative Scotland
towards the publication of this book

Printed by Bell & Bain Ltd, Glasgow

CONTENTS

INTRODUCTION

Most prefaces are, and probably should be, skipped. You've read the first sentence of this one, and are halfway into the second, which supposes you want to know something? Good, an enquiring mind, step in, have a seat. Actually, this preface or introduction is all about you. Whether you're a writer or a reader or a publishing professional with a critical eye for fonts, I'm glad to have your attention.

Did you send something in for consideration? Did you decide against it, not quite knowing how these things work, or up to your ears in self-doubt? Are you lightly jaundiced at finding your own work hasn't made it into this edition? Do you wonder if the so-called Editors are the kind of people you'd trust to appreciate what you write, anyway? Perhaps you experience mulishness and indignation and sorrow about the lack of appreciation for what you are writing? Suspect you'll be infuriated by the things you do see here, that in your opinion are – ha! – not as cool, or zeitgeisty, or intelligent, as your kind of thing, not as brilliant as your story about that seal or walrus or whatever it was that was in the news which appeared to you as a perfect metaphor for a fable about our endangered world and political discourse and the general state of everything, which you laboured over for four days and nights without even breaking to tweet about it . . . ? Good, good, let's talk about that, all of that.

The so-called Editors – you're right, that's what we're called! We read everything, two huge boxes full. My arithmetic is feeble, but say 400-plus contributors, say an average of nine pages per author, that's . . . a lot. We swap boxes. We read the rest. We scribble notes. This process takes about four months, during the winter hibernation. Then, in spring, we meet in a room with all the manuscripts and lists and notes, and a selection of biscuits to fuel the conversation. By this time we have each made a longlist – mine was very long – of perhaps fifty or sixty pieces of work, which have been read twice or thrice. We find out which things appear on our separate longlists, and make a shortlist and cheer out loud that we've got some choices in common. We dig back into the 'maybe' pile, just to be sure we haven't missed a gem. We pull those manuscripts out of their piles and read them again, and swap over and read another. We talk about each piece for some time. We make more lists. We work out a balance of things each of us 'would fight to have in the book' if the other didn't like it. Luckily, no fisticuffs occur, because – and here's the secret magic of it all – as the list tightens up, the stories and poems which remain are the ones we have now read and talked about so much we really admire them, sometimes even love them. As 'Editors', but also as writers, and as readers. The story or poem has done its work if, after all that inspection, it still shines.

We – your so-called Editors – become happy curators of your work, ambassadors, your support team. We have done all of this without changing a word of what you sent, because we don't do any copy-editing – we can't write to you and say *there's a little problem with para 1 on page 3, if you could alter that phrasing we'd like the story better* – nope. Can't do that. This is often the reason why things that are in fact exciting, promising (I'm not using these phrases sarcastically or as jargon), startling or ingenious in concept, may not make the final list. Spelling. Layout. Syntax. A fizzling out of energy. All important. All the responsibility of the author.

You've heard this before but it's true and worth repeating. We all go through our own learning process, developing idiosyn-cratic voices, and it takes time, and the matching up of ideas and the ability to make them work well enough that a total stranger, reading it several times, will find no reason to reject it. That's the skill you're aiming for along the way, always. That never stops. At whatever stage in our personal progress, our work can become overwritten, self-conscious, pedantic, descriptive without enough story, or so plotty that it may lack character. There can be not-short-not-really-stories that are more like the middle of a novel, or poems that flash up the slimmest aspect of a natural event, which hold themselves back, which do not want to be understood, or even met halfway.

And even then, yes, it's competitive. There aren't so many places which will pay you for new work, with no entry fee, which will showcase you when your name has yet to ring bells in reviewing circles. It's worth a bit of risk, for that. *New Writing Scotland* serves a very good purpose, in a very egalitarian way. If you read other people's writing (you do, don't you?) and put yourself in their shoes (you can, can't you?) you might come to agree that it is a literary project which is inclusive and un-snobbish about language or class or any of the other things a New Writer worries about. Or an Old Writer, who's writing new things, and wants to keep writing. Or a Middle-Aged Writer, for that matter.

Where was I? Ah yes. Have I alleviated any of your anxieties? What are the rules, again, you say? You'll find them on page ix, immediately after this Introduction. The rules for submission – but I dislike that word. Why submit? Just offer. Just push it into an envelope which lands on our desk and let us look at it. There is no humiliation involved in these things. Rejection? Ouch. But . . . accept failure as a condition of the work. Write something else. Keep your hands moving.

And – now this is exciting – the editors change! They revolve. Evolve. Devolve. Next year will be my final stint as so-called Ed, and then someone new will sit on the edge of the desk and eat those biscuits with the excellent Samuel Tongue, and have those conversations about your writing. S/he will have different experiences and tastes and views and interests and erogenous zones for wordplay. Behind the scenes, in the small back room, there are the permanent staff of ASLS, the crew of the mothership, who do the unglamorous work of logging and tracking all the texts you send, attaching numbers, checking for lost pages. Necessary and exacting labour.

Have I forgotten about you, the casual browser of bookshops or snooper of other people's shelves? No. I'm delighted you've read this far and would love you to keep reading, in any order or disorder that takes your fancy. Everything is arranged alphabetically (by surname) which creates an interesting set of juxtapositions designed to amuse, challenge, intrigue. Put on your best clothes to read. Or take them all off. Dive, tiptoe, hurdle your way into it as you please.

How about you, the publishing professional? The writing tutor? The 'other half' of someone who writes poetry, to whom you wish to lend encouragement? You, the parent of a wordy child? The granny of a rapper-rhymer called Tom? The far-flung relative who picks up this copy in a back-packing hostel and feels a tug towards home, the familiar shorelines, the weather of yesterdays and the sound of tourists complaining about the midges? There is something in this collection for all of you – although I don't think, this year, we did get anything featuring a walrus.

Susie Maguire

NEW WRITING SCOTLAND 37: SUBMISSION INSTRUCTIONS

The thirty-seventh volume of *New Writing Scotland* will be published in summer 2019. Submissions are invited from writers resident in Scotland or Scots by birth, upbringing or inclination. All forms of writing are welcome: autobiography and memoirs; creative responses to events and experiences; drama; graphic artwork (monochrome only); poetry; political and cultural commentary and satire; short fiction; travel writing or any other creative prose may be submitted, but not full-length plays or novels, though self-contained extracts are acceptable. The work must not be previously published, submitted, or accepted for publication elsewhere, and may be in any of the languages of Scotland.

Submissions should be typed on one side of the paper only and the sheets secured at the top left corner. Prose pieces should be double-spaced and carry an approximate word-count. **You should provide a covering letter, clearly marked with your name and address.** *Please also put your name on the individual works.* If you would like to receive an acknowledgement of receipt of your manuscript, please enclose a stamped addressed postcard. If you would like to be informed if your submission is unsuccessful, or would like your submissions returned, you should enclose a stamped addressed envelope with sufficient postage. Submissions should be sent by **30 September 2018**, in an A4 envelope, to the address below. We are sorry but we cannot accept submissions by email.

Please be aware that we have limited space in each edition, and therefore shorter pieces are more suitable – although longer items of exceptional quality may still be included. **Please send no more than four poems, or one prose work**. Successful contributors will be paid at the rate of £20 per published page. Authors retain all rights to their work(s), and are free to submit and/or publish the same work(s) elsewhere after they appear in *New Writing Scotland*.

ASLS
Scottish Literature
7 University Gardens
University of Glasgow
Glasgow G12 8QH, Scotland
Tel +44 (0)141 330 5309
www.asls.org.uk

Patricia Ace

TALKING TO CANCER

In the insomniac nights of mid-life
the conversations with cancer begin.

Fuck you! is my starter for ten.
My friends and I line up like ducks

in the shooting gallery of genes and luck
as the test results return surely

as rowboats on our childhood lakes:
Come in number 3, your time is up!

There's a new set of euphemisms to learn:
mass for tumour, *quality of life, respite.*

My friends lose hair, lose weight;
shuffle in robes like Buddhist monks.

Meanwhile, our parents don't know
who we are any more; need round-the-clock

care or fester on dementia wards for years.
Take them! I tell cancer. But cancer

has no truck with the frail and old.
Cancer blocks its ears and won't be told.

2

Juliet Antill

A NIGHT IN FERMANAGH

She welcomed us in, showed us the room
with twin beds and dark-papered walls.
Donegal was just over the border. In between
lay the fast-greening flesh of the land
where cows bellowed like car alarms.
The bath was down the corridor.
Our host described proper use of hot water
and thanked God for saving the power.

How we shook the boards that night,
how we rattled the Virgin Mary! (Just as earlier
the afternoon had rattled out thunderstorms.)
She knew of course, in the morning, the way
she regarded us, as she brought us our eggs
with the quivering yolks; we, her sole exhibit:
a pair of grotesques, ravenous, un-slept,
not a ring to show between us (yours
in a pocket ready to toss in Lough Erne).

After we left, no doubt, the woman
crossed herself as she stripped the beds
and straightened the Virgin –
Mary still with a beatific smile.

Douglas Bruton

WALK DON'T RUN

When a girl, my grandmother gutted fish. She has black-and-white photographs in wooden frames on either side of the mantelpiece clock, the pictures turning yellow, pictures of her standing with other fish-gutting girls whose names she chanted to me when I was a child. In the pictures she's fourteen, my grandmother then looking like me now. The girls are outside in the pictures, the sky grey above them and the thick arms of fishermen at their waists, the sculpted folds of their skirts hiding their legs. They're all smiles, the young men and the girls. One of the men might be my grandfather, though he died before I was born so I do not recognise his smile, not like I recognise hers and all its uncertainty. Her name was Julia then, my grandmother, and Julia is my name now.

My grandmother told me once, about the fish, about the sharp knife slicing into the soft underbelly, sliding mouth to tail, and then scooping out the shit and the slime-slippy guts, a pink black mess that the gulls screamed and fought over. She used that word: shit. I remember looking across at my mam to see if she'd heard it too and to make sure it was all right to be still listening. My grandmother's voice did not falter as she told of the fish packed in ice or salt and loaded onto carts and driven to shops and hotels in places she could name then – but not now. And afterwards the fish-silver on the palms of her hands, and she a fisherman's bride. Too soon, she once said, too soon a bride; I did not know why it was too soon.

Now she's old, her fingers turned into knots in her shallow lap, folded there like the curled legs of dead spiders or like the clutched feet of dead birds. And her skin dark, like old wood. I have to look after her some days. I should love her, but she's old and never speaks, not like before when I was a child at her knee adrift in her stories. She sits in a high-backed armchair, one of her eyes cloudy like the eye of a grilled fish, the other watching the world moving around her. And she does not speak.

I have to look after her, most weekends, days when I'd rather be smoking cigarettes with Johnny at the café, holding his interest, one too many of my blouse buttons undone and mam's disapproval a voice in the back of my head. And Johnny not leaving my side and saying nice things to me. Only I'm here with my grandmother, watching the clock on the mantelpiece counting down the minutes and the hours of my day, the minutes and hours of her day.

She sleeps mostly, in her chair, her head tilted back like a child's and her mouth slack, open so that I can see her teeth, not straight and not white. I counted them once, her teeth, when she slept. Nine on the bottom and eight on the top. It didn't seem enough to me. She smells of lavender and roses, and underneath faintly still of fish, I think, the smell catching in my nostrils and at the back of my throat so that I almost retch.

When she wakes she doesn't talk. At least I never understand the sounds that she makes. I ask her if she wants a cup of tea and from her reply I cannot guess if she does or she doesn't, so I don't always bother. I stay till six and then someone else takes over: sometimes my dad, sometimes my mam. They're never late, and I should be grateful for that.

'Did you talk to her?' my mam always asks.

And I do talk to her, even though I'm not sure she hears. I tell my grandmother stuff, things I wouldn't tell anyone else, secrets of sorts. Even if she does hear I know that she will not tell, not ever. It's like talking to myself, like thinking my thoughts out loud. I told her about Dad and the woman next door, how I caught him with his hand under her skirt when he was supposed to be helping her with her decorating, and the look on her pinched face and the sound that she made, like she couldn't breathe. They didn't know I was watching, quiet, through a crack in the door, come to tell Dad there was someone on the phone for him.

I have to dust and clean while I'm at my grandmother's house, wash any dishes that get dirtied and keep everything just so. It doesn't take much of my time. There's just my grandmother and she never moves from the chair, not unless I help her. I take her to the toilet several times a day, just in case. Not the upstairs one, never upstairs now. Even her bed has been moved down to the ground-floor spare room. I take her, supporting her arm and moving so slow I sometimes think we aren't moving at all. I lock the door from the inside even though there's only us. The air in there is sickly sweet with air freshener, something with the thick sticky scent of freesias hanging in it. I steady her in front of the toilet, lift her dress, ease her pants to her ankles, and sit her down. It was something she used to do for me when I was little, it is something the same but different now that she's the smaller of us. I sit on the edge of the bath and talk to her until she's finished.

I tell my grandmother about Mr Jamieson at school and him standing so close to me that we were touching, and his breath like sour milk and the other kids in the class passing whispers back and forth, giving shape to stories that never were. He's old, Mr Jamieson. Not so old as my grandmother, but there's grey in his hair, salt-and-pepper grey, thicker just at the sides. And hair grows out of his nose and out of his ears. Joan, a girl I talk to sometimes, once sent him a Valentine card, just for laughs. He pinned it up on the board beside his desk and kept it there all year. By the end the laugh was on Joan and she blushed every time she was in his class, until he took it down.

When my grandmother is finished, I pull off a length of toilet paper and fold it into a padded mitten around my hand. Then I wipe her, there between her legs. If I told the girls at school they'd make faces of disgust and I'd admit to them that I don't know how anyone could. But I do it, and it's no different to wiping clean the kitchen surfaces now that I'm used to it. Then I pull up her pants and she shifts her weight from one hip to the other to help, like a slow dance or a fish wriggling its very last. I wash her hands and mine, then dry them, and unlock the door and walk one careful half-step at a time back to her armchair in the living room.

She knows I smoke, my grandmother; she knows, but my mam doesn't. Sometimes I imagine my grandmother telling me not to, giving me advice like she did when I was very young, my grandmother's hand on my arm, keeping me back – always look both ways before crossing the road, and never run with scissors in your hand, or a knife. Now it is getting warmer again I go out into my grandmother's back garden, stand by the open window so I can still see her, and I light up. Every now and then I ask if she's okay and I think she nods a little. And I tell her what it's like outside, on the other side of the glass.

The daffodils are fit to burst into colour, the swollen ends bent like the heads of diving birds and showing yellow beneath the green. The snowdrops have melted away and the air is hung with birdsong, one child-blown whistle laid on top of another. The tufted grass needs cutting and weeds are beginning to spill out of the borders. My dad'll do the gardening soon, during the Easter holidays, my grandmother's garden getting more attention than our own. And the trees at the bottom of the garden are sticky with buds. I remind her of the jars of pussy willow we used to set on the windowsill in her kitchen, and the sprays of blossom from the flowering cherry and how they went quickly limp and brown at the edges and the water turned green.

At eleven o'clock I bring her tea and some biscuits. Two chocolate digestives on a small side plate. I break each biscuit into four and feed them to her a piece at a time, and I hold the cup to her lips so she can drink.

I tell her what I am getting for Mam's birthday. Mam wants a coffee-making machine, one of those silver ones with black plastic buttons and attachments for making cappuccinos like you get in the coffee shops. I've saved up the money they've paid me for looking after Grandmother at weekends. Four pounds an hour, I get. My dad thought I should do it for nothing, that looking after my grandmother was a duty. I thought he should put his hand under Mam's skirt and not the skirt of the lady next door and that was something like a duty, too.

For a moment there I thought she laughed, my grandmother. Not out loud, not what you would call a laugh, but a soft gargle in her throat, as though she was swallowing something she hadn't chewed properly. I wipe a silver thread of spittle from the corner of her mouth and feed her another quarter piece of biscuit.

Sometimes we sit with the television on. My mam said my grandmother likes to watch the news, so we watch the news. My mam is still pretty for all her years and she looks like my grandmother in the black-and-white pictures. They say I look like her too, but I think they just want me to believe that, so that I feel part of something, part of them. She wears her clothes too tight, Mam does, so tight you can see that she has put on weight. Her hair's brittle and the colour of old rope. It's not her own colour, but it suits her. She works in the supermarket at the end of our street, on the checkouts. I couldn't do that, couldn't listen all day to the sound of the till scanner, insistent like the cheeping of an ignored bird. That's why Mam's put on weight, because she just sits all day. She takes a cushion with her for her back.

At lunchtime I heat soup from a can, a mixture of lentil and tomato, half and half. I warm it up in a battered aluminium pan, not too hot, not so hot that it'll burn her mouth. Mam says I should make her sit at the table, but that's too much trouble. I arrange a tea towel over her front and feed her there in the living room.

I ask my grandmother questions sometimes. Is the soup just as she likes it? Does she want some bread with it? Shall I turn the television up? She nods to everything, at least I make believe that she does. I don't think she really understands. Was Grandfather a good man? Was he gentle with her? And tender? Like a lover in the books my mam reads?

I tell my grandmother all about Johnny at the café. He's gentle, sometimes, when we're alone in the park. He's almost seventeen, three years older than me. He says I'm a looker. He whispers my name in my ear, his breath warm on my neck. And he kisses me – on my cheeks at first, his hands cupping my face and his eyes open. I ask my grandmother if that was what it was like when she was a fish-gutter and Grandfather was a young man on a boat with the sea in his hair and 'Julia' a taste in his mouth. I ask her if Grandfather's kisses are something she remembers still, his lips pressed to hers, and the roughness of his chin that has not seen the razor for two days. Johnny puts his tongue in my mouth sometimes. It does not make me sick. And once, his hand was under my blouse, touching my tits, squeezing them so that they hurt a little. I asked my grandmother if Grandfather ever did that to her, if he ever put his hands between her legs, inside her pants. I told Johnny no, and he swore and took away his kisses. I couldn't bear that, not having him kissing me in the dark of the park, his breath on my neck and my name soft as a prayer on his lips.

My grandmother sleeps again in the late afternoon. I'm talking to her and she sleeps through what I have to say. I tell her again about Dad and the woman next door, and her face screwed as though she was in pain, only I know from the sounds that she made that she was not hurting. And Dad's hand there, as Johnny's hand was under my skirt. Johnny said it was normal, that everybody did it. I heard Joan talking about it to someone at school, talking to Deborah, or Chrissie who smokes where the teachers can see her. I tried not to listen. Johnny said maybe I was just a child. I didn't like it when he said that. He swore again and left me to walk home on my own. But the next day he said he was sorry and that he loved me. It would be okay, he said.

I have put my own hand there. In the dark of my room, not yet asleep and my hand there where Johnny's wanted to be, my fingers wet, slime-slippy like I was gutting fish, only warm. And my breath fast and the air hissing through my teeth, like the woman next door with Dad's hand beneath her skirt.

I ask my sleeping grandmother if she ever did it, if it was as Johnny said, just normal. I am not sure. I say so. The words thin into nothing and the ticking of the clock calls my attention. It's almost six.

Next time I think I'll let him, I say. It's a decision of sorts. Then he won't swear and I won't walk home alone. I say that out loud. But she's not asleep, my grandmother. Her hand reaches for me – the hand that once gutted a million fish settles on my arm, and I look at her face and she's crying.

I ask her what's wrong and she mutters something. Her lips move and I lean in close, only I don't really hear. I wipe the tears from her face with the flat of my hand – silver in my palm now – and I tell her it's all right, that I am here. I tell her my name just in case she's confused, my name which was her name once. I feel the weight of her hand on my arm, a bird-weight, light like something remembered. And I hear again the words of advice that she gave me as a child: always look both ways before crossing the road and never run with scissors in your hand, or a knife. And I don't understand, but somehow her words make sense still.

Becky Carnaffin

MY SISTER LIVES IN A COUNCIL FLAT

My sister lives in a council flat. Ninth floor, right at the top. I visit her once a week. There's a lift, but I always take the stairs. It worries me, her on her own up there. She's isolated. She struggles. I try to tell people this, the council, the social work, but they don't listen. So I visit, once a week. It takes me a while to get there, it's not easy, but she's my sister, and if I don't look out for her, who will?

She was in a good mood the last time I saw her. She made me a cup of tea. The flat was a midden, but less of a midden than usual. I managed to get in the front door without falling over something. There was a clear path along the hall, to the living room, the kitchen, the bathroom, the bedroom. I remarked upon the improved state of the flat to my sister, and she was pleased that I'd noticed. She seemed brighter, more together. I felt hope for the first time in a while. I'd forgotten what it felt like.

*

My sister lives in a council flat. Ninth floor, right at the top. There's a lift, but it smells, so I always take the stairs. I have a key to let myself into the flat. We had a scare a couple of years ago. She wouldn't let me in, I had to call the police, tell them she'd taken an overdose. She denied it, of course, when the police arrived. But they found empty pill packets in the bathroom, so she was taken off in an ambulance. When they let her out, I convinced her that if she gave me a key, it would never happen again. She would be safe.

There's always a moment of apprehension when I put the key in the lock. What will I find on the other side? But today, I'm more relaxed. There was an improvement the last time, things are looking up. The feeling doesn't last long. The door only opens a few inches. I have to put all my weight on it to open it wide enough for me to squeeze through. A burst of sound comes from the living room. A new sound. The hallway is littered again, even worse than usual, I have to pick my way around things to get to the living room. My sister is sitting on the sofa and next to her is a girl. Late teens, early twenties? The girl has red hair, like scarlet red, she has a nose piercing and she's wearing this skimpy top that leaves nothing to the imagination. My sister and her are laughing. I wonder what they're laughing at. Then I realise. They're laughing at me.

'Sorry,' my sister says, in between gulps. 'This is Lauren.'

'Nice to meet you,' the girl says.

*

My sister lives in a council flat. Ninth floor, right at the top, in the kind of building that could never pretend to be anything other than a block of council flats. Mum died a while back, long before my sister moved in. In a way, I'm glad. Mum would have found it difficult, a daughter of hers in a place like that.

The girl's there again the next time I visit. She's doing something in the kitchen. Her hair is blue this time. My sister is in the living room, sat on the sofa, holding a baby and singing to it.

'Are you sure you should be doing that?' I ask my sister.

'What?' she says. 'Singing?'

'Holding the baby.'

'It's fine,' the girl says. I didn't see her come into the living room.

'Is that your child?' I ask her.

'Her name's Khaleesi,' my sister says.

'Where was she last week? When you two were here, who was looking after her?'

'She was with her granny,' the girl says, 'at the park. You ask a lot of questions.'

'We're cleaning the bathroom,' I say to my sister.

'No, we're not,' she says.

'Why not?'

'I'm busy.'

'I brought the bleach with me.'

'I don't like bleach.'

'I carried it all the way up those stairs. Do you know how heavy this stuff is?'

'If she says she doesn't like bleach, she doesn't like bleach,' the girl says. 'It's her flat, not yours.'

*

My sister lives in a council flat. Ninth floor, right at the top. I've told the council, the social work, I'm not happy with her being there. It's not the right environment for her. She's vulnerable. She needs something more secure.

The next time I visit, I take black bin bags. I don't like doing this, but it's necessary. My sister would drown in stuff if it weren't for me, all those pointless ugly things. Mess on the outside, mess on the inside, that's what Mum always said. I let myself in quietly. It's just her in. It's nearly lunch time, but she's still in her pyjamas.

'What are you doing here?' she says.

I don't answer her. I just open one of the bin bags and start picking things off the floor and putting them in. A magazine, a soft toy, a candle holder.

'Stop it,' my sister says.

A pack of tissues, a scarf, a cassette tape, a notebook, a box of paints.

'Stop it,' she says again, crying now.

I see the dog ornament sitting on the shelf. I've always despised that thing. It's cheap and nasty.

'No,' she shouts as I reach for it. She lunges forward and we've both got our hands around it, pulling hard. Then it falls, smashes on the floor. And I laugh. I don't mean to, it just comes out. There's a hand on my arm, nails digging in, pulling me backwards, out of the living room, along the hall. It's the girl. It happens so quickly I don't have time to fight back. She shoves me out of the flat and slams the door in my face. My sister's flat. My sister.

*

You wouldn't think it to look at us now, but when we were younger, people thought we were twins. We were born in the same year, but we're not twins. In the week after I was born, Mum had an uncharacteristic moment of carelessness, and nine months later my sister arrived. We shared a bedroom when we were growing up. I was always tidy, nothing was ever out of place. My sister was the opposite. She was incapable of keeping her things in her half of the room, they always spread into my half. Whenever Mum walked into our bedroom, what she saw was mess everywhere. She didn't see my neatly folded clothes. She didn't see my tidy bed.

*

I ring the police later that day. I wait till the bruises have shown up properly on my arm, it's important to get these things right. It only takes them a few minutes to arrive. A policeman and a policewoman.

'That was quick,' I say.

'Were you expecting us?' the policeman says.

'Of course,' I say. 'Has someone gone up there? Is she safe? Is my sister safe, has that woman been . . .'

I don't finish my sentence. The policeman's folded his arms and the policewoman's eyebrows are raised.

'I don't think you understand,' the policewoman says. 'Your sister called us. That's why we're here.'

*

My sister lives in a council flat. I don't see her now.

Jim Carruth

BRINGING IN THE COWS

There are days when you come to fetch them
and they are nowhere to be seen.
The brae empty of cattle offers a blank face.

Your hope is that they stand somewhere
beyond the rise of the field
that stretches on down to the marsh.

You send the dog up and over the ridge
so he too disappears from view
and you are left with nothing to bring home.

More and more urgent each command given
to send the dog left and right
and away back across a field out of sight.

Though you whistle or shout until hoarse
the hill offers not one word back
no bark or bellow and all seems lost.

You are searching for what you cannot see
seeking the return of that
which might already have disappeared.

You long for one strong thick head
rising above the crest
a signal for the rush of the herd to come.

Lynn Davidson

LEAVING BASS ROCK GANNET COLONY

After skypointing to show
it's ready

after one last dive, shorting the sea
(the crack, the pressured current fizzing)

after one last moment of great aloneness: a fleck
in oceans

after the last fish in its gut –
the fin and skin and bone of it – tears apart

it takes a final flight, blowing
Bass Rock into the feathery pieces   we call

aura or
atoms   we called

father or
Adam

Beth Frieden

A' SIREADH THAIBHSEAN AIR TRÀIGH
A' BHÀIGH SHIAR, BHÀTARSAIGH

Oidhche Shamhna gun ghealach, a' ghainmheach
a' cagarsaich air a' bhruaich. Cùl ri
cùl, fosgailte agus dùinte, roinn sinn
paidhir mhiotagan, is ghluais sinn a
dh'ionnsaigh langanaich na mara, ise
na cuthach air fàire, a' sireadh an

dealachaidh a bu dual rinn eadar
a' mhuir agus an tràigh. Sheas sinn ann am
fianais a' cheòth' a' tarraing anail,
a' tabhainn ar saoghail airson geasachd, ged
nach rachadh a h-aithneachadh. Bhioraich sinn
ach cha do bhioraich an Grioglachan.

Chùm sinn oirnn ag èisteachd ann, agus
ghlan na rionnagan sinn len solas fann.

MUC-MHARA

Nuair a nochdas i, bidh thu air a
gairm iomadh turas nad chridhe, is
fhathast thig iongnadh ort mar thonn. Is e
mìorbhail a th' innte is a tha na fonn.

Cuiridh i cèilidh ort, gad bhrosnachadh
airson cò aig' a tha fios ach ma tha
ise ann, agus beò, agus fìor, dè
nach gabh a dhèanamh? A' mhuc-mhara,

a cuideam gràsmhor gun chuideam, cho caomh,
cho trang, a' beannachadh a' chuain le
siubhal, na h-eileamaid fhèin, cho saillte
ris na deòir thaingeil a thig dhad shùilean

nuair a nochdas i a-rithist
nad chuimhne, bliadhnaichean às dèidh a teachd.

Harry Giles

THE WORKER

The worker is unhappy.

The worker is taking a mid-morning shower and assessing her life, her work, and whether it can continue.

The worker cannot explain her job to a taxi driver, but she is so busy, so busy: this is what she says when asked how she is, *so busy*.

The worker's busy working life consists mostly of emails: she emails to pitch for work; she responds to emails soliciting her work; to do her work, she emails people to ask them to do work; sometimes she sends longer emails containing advice, ideas and spreadsheet attachments.

The worker, in between emails, checks Twitter, the hashtag #fullcommunism, which is what she tweets when she is unhappy, which is always: 'Ran out of hot water half-way through my shower #fullcommunism'; 'When will the nights start getting shorter? #fullcommunism now'; '#fullcommunism with a three hour delay on the morning chorus as a transitional demand'.

The worker is aware that the disjuncts between her ironic deployment of radical political terminology, the record of totalitarian state violence under the same terminology and the clear need for revolutionary political change are, at the very least, problematic, but these disjuncts ease her horror, which is acute.

The worker does not know how to properly and responsibly account for the relationship between, on the one hand, the immediacy of her acute horror, and, on the other, horror on a global political scale; that is to say, she is gnawed by the question of whether her acute and terrible horror – which manifests as purely psychological, though arguably it has a firm material basis, insofar as the material and the psychological can be disentangled, insofar as they are not, in the immediacy of her own acute, terrible and unbearable horror, entirely co-constituted – whether this acute, terrible, unbearable but deeply solipsistic horror can be compared to or accounted for by the same socioeconomic formulations as disease, famine, war and death.

The worker is rinsing conditioner from her hair, and then realises she has already done so, and so is rinsing already-rinsed hair, which at this moment strikes her as a metaphor so gruesome she has to lean on the tiles to catch her breath.

The worker does not have a job.

The worker gets paid irregularly for a range of tasks encompassing management, consultation and creative development; she has two degrees and last year her total income after business expenses was less than the minimum wage.

The worker frequently spends the morning sobbing.

The worker frequently spends the afternoon in bed numbed by those American drama serials, pirated on her high-speed WiFi, which offer that precisely engineered balance between *clever* and *stupid* which enables immersive escapism without an excess of blank rage.

The worker is not clear as to how she is able to afford high-speed WiFi and a thick duvet on her objectively insufficient income, and yet she can; perhaps it is because she does not have children; perhaps it is because she barely eats.

The worker draws on scraps of paper small and precise sketches
of urban wildlife, and these creative interludes are what
the worker uses to justify her life: there are moments
of drawing in which 'peace' is something more than an
abstract noun.

The worker's parents own their own house outright.

The worker does not live there.

The worker values her independence.

The worker has had her eyes closed for the last five minutes, enjoying
the sense of nullity that comes from falling water; she keeps
her eyes closed.

The worker took an old friend to the pub last night – an old friend,
it should be said, whom the worker has always wanted to
sleep with, both in the sense of having sex with and in the
sense of entering several hours of warm oblivion with, but
who through a thousand signals has made it clear they do
not find the worker sexually attractive, at least according
to the worker's understanding, which cannot encompass
the thought that anyone would find her attractive, raising the
question of whether the signals are transmitted or merely
received, a question that is nonetheless moot given the
impossibility of acting on any of its possible answers – and
explained at length to that friend in the pub how all of her
work, the emails, the emails about emails, was an elaborate
mechanism for providing economic support to those ex-
periments in drawing which provide her only respite from
'the screaming'.

The worker said, 'I want to be an artist,' and her friend said, 'You
are one already,' and the worker said, 'No.'

The worker believes firmly in the necessity of a strong welfare state, and perhaps even in the strategic facility of a Universal Basic Income in order to provide a base level of comfort and security to every human individual so that they are better able to pursue their self-fulfilment, except insofar as it applies to herself; that is to say, the worker will happily attend a protest march in defence of doctors' salaries (this is not true, she will not be happy on attending, she will be anxious and afraid, but she will still attend), but cannot imagine defending herself; that is to say, the worker is fervent about fighting for the happiness of every individual on the planet except for herself.

The worker is aware of this, and was aware of this when she explained to her friend that the only thing that would make her feel more vain, more self-indulgent, more useless to society than her current work would be calling herself an 'artist'.

The worker's friend held the worker's arm.

The worker experiences instances when she can locate her potential for happiness within a coherent political discourse: the moment when her friend held the worker's arm was one such.

The worker's friend, with extraordinary gentleness, let go.

The worker opens her eyes and turns off the shower and stands very still, with her body held open, dripping.

The worker's contracts are not regular.

The worker does not have a pension or sick leave.

The worker begins to shiver as the water evaporates from her skin.

The worker has friends who refer to this form of work as 'precarious,' but she is suspicious of this terminology, uncertain as to whether it is truly a different labour system to that of the nineteenth-century industrial working class on whom Marxist economics was predicated.

The worker's increasing shivering causes her to bend at the knees.

The worker returns often to a mental image of anonymous hordes of men in flat caps queueing or perhaps swarming outside factory gates, waiting for work, and compares that image to an image of her inbox.

The worker understands that she should step out of the shower, and though the distance between 'shivering' and 'stepping out of the shower' is impossible, there is somewhere a voice reminding the worker to count her breaths.

The worker wonders whether 'precarity' is the name that people with middle-class backgrounds and training give to their situation in order to emotionally distance themselves from those swarming men and their forms of struggle, and so whether the defining characteristic of contemporary precarity is simply that its workers have been promised an exit which has never appeared, and indeed several of the worker's friends refer to themselves as 'precarious workers' when the worker knows for a fact that they have a savings account, wealthy parents or at least a university-grade education which has granted them the verbal facility to successfully negotiate the world's financial tortures far in excess of that usually afforded to what the worker thinks of as the 'real' working class, whom the worker rarely meets.

The worker said as much last night in the pub to her friend, who fell silent.

The worker remembered then, with a burst of psychic pain, that her
    friend had wealthy parents with whom they did not speak,
    could not speak since those parents' refusal to accept their
    'lifestyle'.

The worker, at that moment, turned back to her friend with her lips
    shaking, and the prehistoric terror in the worker's eyes was
    so deep and all-absorbing that her friend bit down their
    anger, shook their head and said, 'It's okay. Really, it's okay.'

The worker counts; the worker counts; the worker counts.

The worker felt that it was not okay, and would never be okay.

The worker felt herself at that point in the conversation launching
    into a familiar cycle of self-loathing, aware that her level of
    self-loathing and her ability to project that self-loathing
    onto others was itself loathsome, but also unable to turn
    that awareness towards overcoming self-loathing, meaning
    that that awareness was itself a source of further loathing,
    and that any attempt to explain this to her friend would
    also be a manifestation of that self-loathing and further
    reason to be loathed.

The worker thus, after a frail extension of the conversation in which
    she attempted to comfort her friend for her friend's inability
    to provide true comfort without verbally acknowledging
    that either of them required or was asking for comfort from
    the other, hugged her friend and went home, turning the
    corner before she began to cry.

The worker, counting, steps out of the shower and reaches for her
    towel.

The worker believes that her brightest times of all have been those
    when she has been able to construe her horror (acute, terrible,

unbearable, insurmountable) as a product of 'neoliberalism', when she has been able to blame neoliberalism for the destruction of geographically local community, perpetuation of a state of permanent terror and anxiety, dependence on chronic debt, complicity in international warfare, constant forms of normative violence and overall atmosphere of dread which, combined, are the cause of the horror which is at this moment threatening her life.

When the worker can identify the cause of her suffering as political, the worker can imagine being able to do something about it, even if the action of 'doing something about it' is permanently out of reach, and even if the recurring realisation that political change may be out of reach causes that moment of clarity to collapse back into self-loathing.

In this moment, however, hanging her towel on the radiator and pulling on a t-shirt and shorts, that instant of hope provides the worker with enough impetus for her to sit at her desk, open her laptop and get to work.

Brian Hamill

THINKING THESE THOUGHTS

She is lying on the bed. Head and shoulders raised by three pillows.

A notepad is on the night-stand. A pen. The pen has purple ink. It is for a child, a wee one, a baby, and so anything written in it would look like the outpourings of a toddler.

She would be embarrassed to use it.

Outside the light beginning to fade. Bright evenings will make for the blackest of nights. This is true. Her head nodding, slightly. From the position she's in, she can see a square of sky, mostly cloud. Those wee ruffly clouds, white and tapering at the edges. There is a name for clouds of that sort, but she doesn't remember it. Cumulus is a type of cloud, she is sure of that at least. She will say these are cumulus clouds, even if this is not true. Visible is a square of sky, cumulus clouds, the roof of the building opposite, brown tiles, two chimneys, a few windows on its top row. This is all.

The room is becoming dim. A light should be put on. Already the corners of the room in darkness. The curtains too, like for a child's bed. Also purple. And a repeating pattern of yellow dogs with bones in their mouths. While smiling. Some of them upside down.

She listens. Thinking. Hands are resting on her stomach.

Is it a story?

That she is here. Lying down. That she is thinking these thoughts. That outside there are cumulus clouds. That every now and then, somebody appears in one of the windows opposite. That it's people she has seen there before. Living their lives. She doesn't know them. The lady with the black hair. The man. Older. That they move around their room as they talk. Always moving, always talking. Sometimes she throws things at him, cushions, water from her glass. If it is water. Probably it isn't. Sometimes he shouts back, the wide-open mouth can be seen even from where she is, all the way across the street. That they are mental. The both of them.

No, it is not. Nothing is happening here. In here. And nothing keeps on happening.

It could be a painting. But she can't paint. Not at all. Not even anything.

If something was to happen, it could form a story for her.

Things are happening, elsewhere. Her window is open slightly, and sounds come in. Sounds are caused by happenings. People passing by her house. The house she lives in currently. Footsteps and if she listens hard, sometimes the noise of a dog's paws alongside. People and things pass. They go on. Their voices too.

If a painting was done from outside the house. From on the roof opposite. Her head against the pillow, it would be small and dark there, round, with the brown hair spilling out, the room grey and silent, her face not distinct at all, no features except maybe shadows at the eyes, where they delve into the skull, just a round area of skin, the different colour, lying there, as if peeking out above the window frame. The painting would show the street below, with the people passing. In the moment being painted, maybe one old man with a yellow dog. He would be saying things to the dog in a soft voice as it softly pisses against the lamp post out there, before they go on their way again.

This is no story. Not really.

Why are her thoughts not one? Thoughts are something. The alternative would only be no thoughts . . . would be nothing.

She doesn't want something to have to happen. It would be too easy. To go and force it. Anybody could do so. Anybody. To think of a girl leaving the house, going to the pub at the corner of the road, talking to the barman, and so on. Of course this would lead to, whatever. It is too easy. It takes more to make sure that things don't happen. For not happening to be a thing.

She is wondering what the passing old man's imaginary yellow dog's name is.

Directionless thoughts can become a story. Do become stories. If the step is taken to just state that some event took place in the past. Recent, preferably. But not essentially. That is all. She is on the bed, thinking her directionless thoughts, about the roof she sees from the window, about the clouds, fluffy, aye, cumulus too, about the dog, yellow, bounding past on the pavement while its master follows on behind, smiling – this is a story, because her mother died last week. Nothing more. She is lying on a bed, thinking, and her mother died last week. This is a story.

Just how it is.

Of course, her mother did not die last week. Not ever. Her mother has not died. She is alive – alive! Outlive the rest of us, and so on.

And still she is lying on the bed. Her head and shoulders propped up by the pillows. Three.

The light gradually becoming less and less. The room is close to black. The curtain-dogs just darkened blobs. They are better for it.

It would be a story if she was lying on the bed remembering

something. Something that happened in the room. Something both terrible and dramatic!

The room is close to black, but the walls are painted a bright shade of white. She remembers, from this bed, watching her mother and stepfather argue about the shade of white to use. Chalk or eggshell. The choice was eggshell. Her mother's. She wanted a brightness. Cleanliness and brightness, aye. The walls do look very white, even with the light this dim. Coming on black.

If she was to remember that her stepfather came into the room, white, eggshell, once and sat on the bed and put his hand underneath her t-shirt, and took hold of her there. Then it's a story, then it's a real fucking obvious story, it would be Her Story, capital letters, come on, and maybe folk would like it because of her act of remembering, and of telling it. And if the stepfather might come in and do it again. Her left tit again, not the right. The left being bigger. It is noticeable.

It is nonsensical. The left is not bigger. Not noticeably. And the stepfather would not come in now and do so. She wants to write about the not happening. Not this. It is nonsensical.

And he is away now. The stepfather. She knows she should not think up stuff. Think of stuff. Definitely not stuff such as this.

She does not want to make things into a story. There must be another way. If she could paint, she would paint this from inside the room. Just how it is.

She can't.

It will only be a story if something happens.

There is a sound downstairs. Inside the building this time. The home. Footsteps.

Her hands resting on her stomach. To the tops of her legs. Her dull, stagnant, embarrassing thoughts. Yellow dogs and left tits. She feels like she should apologise.

She needs to have everything clear in her mind, everything that happens now. It is not a story because these things are not happening to her.

The lady is walking past the window right across the expanse of air between that building and this with a cigarette in her mouth and the tiny plume of blue wisping up, the black hair, her top is dark red, a siren in the distance, a very faint siren could be moving further away, laughing below, more than one person, and talking that could also be them or else others nearby on the same pavement outside, birds on the roof opposite, a set of wings flaps up above the lady at the window as she passes, the plume going up too, wings beating, the corners of this room are black now, there is only the view out, the fucking kid's curtains, the purple tinge still visible. A notepad on the night-stand, a pen, what good is that, there are footsteps in this same house a creak like somebody has stepped on a stair
she is trying to think but feels heavy on the bed
so heavy
it is giving way underneath
she is sinking into it
sinking

She can see and hear and feel all of this at the same time. All of it, all in this same second. Nothing sees or hears her. If she could paint, or write. But for her, just to lie, thinking these things.

Something is going to happen. She will just keep on being.

There is movement. There was a yellow dog outside and the woman across the street. Eggshell white. The dog pissed a lamp post. Somebody laughing. This is all she has. God. She should laugh too. Fucking eggshell. It is nonsensical. God.

It is only a story if something was to happen. A creak like someone has stepped on a stair. And the woman across the street – but she has now passed out of sight. If only.

She can't.

Lars Horn

FOREST

Ellie Forest. Photographer. She once said: she'd like to see the people
she knew, see what they were doing at the same time as herself.

Ellie Forest. Thin. Very. Strangely beautiful with it. Only wore
black. Rolled cigarettes one-handed.

Goodbye was not something she said. If you were with her,
everything was lithe and electric; but once she left, she left. Hurt a
lot of people like that, right up to her death.

Cancer. Refused to stop working; one week was all she took off
at the end. Refused to tell anyone either. It was her partner, Peter,
who did that: we got an email, but not a group one, Peter went
through her address book; it took him two months. In the email,
he talked about Ellie, and her death, and he asked for our news. He
attached a photo of her with their two dogs. I didn't know she had
dogs; but then, I did not know emails could feel so soft.

I'm not sure why I'm telling you about this woman. I suppose
because she struck me when I was young, logic would say too young
to understand how one person could have something and another
not. But I don't buy that. I'm not sure age matters that much: if
someone marks you, somehow carves themselves into how you see
life thereafter, it just happens, whatever age you're at. And she had
something: something raw, like exposed cable or a sharp-edged tool.
She wasn't what you'd call easy or safe, but nor was the tide of her
something you'd fight against.

I often think of Ellie: she's still there cutting space, mixing chem-
icals in a makeshift darkroom that time in Wales. The B&B owner
hadn't known what to do when, coming to straighten the sheets, she
found washing lines of prints across the ceiling and the room's light
bulbs changed to red. She'd simply asked if anything would stain,
and Ellie had said: *ach no*, which we all knew was a lie, but she said it
so softly that you forgot she was lying, ended up believing her instead.

I always liked her last name: the 'awayness' of it, and the breadth.
You could walk into that name.

Sandra Ireland

ULTRAMARINE

Trauma can affect the non-verbal
part of the brain. Art can free feelings of loss
and grief and pain from the subconscious,
aiding vocalisation.

He lacks the ordnance of words.
A self-portrait shows
stitches where his mouth should be;
eyes like empty casings.
He left a part of himself
in the desert,
this ultra-Marine,
the part which glows
Tyrian Purple.

Now he is bone black inside;
loaded with dark pigment;
aggregates
to be ground down and
made smooth with linseed words.
Time heals.
Give yourself time.

Time is just a jumbled mix
on his palette;
there was a lot of ochre out there,
and green earth and
sometimes, now he's home,
he feels the trickle
of warm vermilion
seeping into
his boots.

Vicki Jarrett

YELLOWNESS

She takes the long route back from town and detours around the northern fringes of the estate, following the slow coils of pebble-dashed houses. It's not that she's reluctant to reach home. She doesn't want to worry John. He only has her welfare at heart, her *wellness*, as he has taken to calling it.

There are three basic house models on the estate: bungalows with slanted roofs, semi-detached two-storey cubes, and ginger-bread-house chalets with a single upstairs window squeezed under a pointed roof. The houses on this particular avenue back onto a strip of woodland bordering the golf course. That must be a bonus, she thinks. To be able to look out of your kitchen window and not see half a dozen other windows, framing half a dozen other women washing countless other dishes, like staring into some crude infinity mirror. She stops on the pavement between numbers twenty-two and twenty-six, puts down the carrier bag and rubs at the red groove the handle has left across her palm.

It is this house that keeps calling her back.

The front lawn has gone over to foot-high tangles of tussocky grass, weeds and overgrown bushes. A green wheelie bin lies on its side in the driveway, untended remnants of forsythia bearing thin lemony flowers twined around the wheels. Sections of harling have flaked away from the chimney, exposing the brickwork, and there are tiles missing from the apex of the roof, giving it a bitten look. Something illegible has been scrawled on one of the lower window-boards.

She takes a few steps forwards then stops when her foot comes down with a crumpling noise on something hard. An aluminium can, some kind of energy drink, with *monster* printed in titanium-yellow gothic lettering. She glances up, right and left, to make sure no one has heard or seen her but the street is deserted. She picks her way more carefully through the weeds and rubbish, around the back of the house where she knows one of the boards is so rotted

it can be lifted right off the window. But she won't go in right now.
She leaves the bag containing the litre of Hidden Sun emulsion and
a fresh brush tucked behind a geriatric rosehip bush for later.

*

The first time, she'd been following a trail of yellow. Not quite a
yellow brick road but that initial thought, with its attendant cheering
munchkins, had made her smile and that in itself had seemed worth
a follow, or five.

There had been a quality to the light that day. An effect like those
black-and-white images with a single vivid colour: a girl in a red
dress lost in the woods, a gritty New York street with lozenges of
yellow taxicabs, London with a solitary red double-decker bus. The
version she'd been given was damp autumnal Edinburgh, dark stone
and cobbles, a day that never quite reached full daylight, and all the
yellows glowing, as if they'd hoarded away some of the sun's power
precisely for this moment. Yellow grit bins, double yellow lines, street
signs, autumn leaves in migration, some still clinging to black
branches, others slicked to the tarmac, dazzling flurries in mid-air.
At first it had felt like a gift, a beautiful and wholly unexpected gift
from the world to her.

But wait.

She was too young for this, surely? Only old people were enrap-
tured by autumn colours, their years giving them the maturity and
philosophical bent to appreciate the turning of the seasons. But she
wasn't there yet, was she? She stopped and looked straight up into
the murky grey sky. Was there something wrong with her eyesight?
She blinked hard, shook herself all over like a dog, coughed and
narrowed her eyes, walked quicker – enough of this strolling along
like she didn't have anywhere to be. John would be expecting her
back and he would be worried. But still, the yellows continued to
shout out, and with such force. It had to mean something. But what?
Was this a form of communication? From whom? Or what? Was it
rather that the rest of the world was fading away and the yellows
would be the last to go? She was so tired of asking herself questions
and not knowing the answers.

Perhaps, the thought occurred to her then, this visual effect had a purpose, especially in the elderly. The eyes and brain colluded to highlight this specific colour, prompting thoughts about the great cycle of life, death and rebirth. Leaves turning and falling, allowing for new growth in the summer, there was a harmony, a *rightness* to it all. Encouraged by the display of yellows, these thoughts would naturally follow each other, holding hands like the lines of a well-loved nursery rhyme. But she saw the process now for what it was. A trick. A visual prompt to accept mortality with good grace, a pre-programmed opiate to help smother our panic as we mount the steps to the slaughterhouse. Yellow as a warning. The end must be approaching faster than she'd ever imagined.

She began to count her breaths, trying to slow them. She must stop letting her thoughts control her. Instead, she must simply observe them and let them go. This was something John had been patiently trying to explain to her. And he knew what he was talking about, he'd read up on it all when he was off work last month with his low blood pressure. She forced herself to walk at a normal pace. The yellows were beautiful. It was perfectly reasonable to enjoy them.

Breathe. One two three four five slower six Slower seven. Okay. It's okay. Just breathe. And walk.

Perhaps her perception of colour was off-kilter because there was something wrong with her thinking. Was that possible? According to John, it was a mistake to identify too closely with her own thoughts and feelings. She had to learn to let them be and not fixate so much. This sounded ideal but she couldn't help wondering, in that case, where and in what form *she* actually existed. She knew she wasn't her body. That was just a thing. Her brain was another thing, but still not her. So where was she? She had to be somewhere, didn't she? She had a sense of herself as diffuse, fugitive, ghosting the capillaries and passing through echoing ventricles, twisting around bones, slinking behind the eyes, just sometimes. She had no real control over anything. She was a stowaway. If her body breathed out too hard at the wrong moment she might be expelled altogether and simply evaporate into the atmosphere. She imagined herself as a small cloud, dispersing. Could she be her perceptions? Before they turned into thoughts or feelings, a collection of pure sensations, texture, sound, light, colour. That might work.

*

The trail had continued: the canary flag of a For Sale sign, a dog-chewed tennis ball, a run of yellow car registration plates, all of which had led her away from her habitual route home to the south side of the estate, where John would be waiting. The thought of him tugged at her and she paused. As she deliberated, a blackbird landed a few feet ahead on the pavement, cocked his head and regarded her with a bright eye, ringed with gold. But not only ringed, she realised. The bird's eye socket was like a tiny golden cup and the colour went all the way behind the eye too. Perhaps it stretched right back to the bird's brain, lighting it up like a miniature sun, blazing away unseen inside its feathered head. The blackbird led her on, in a series of short flights, tree to hedge to fence to driveway, his beak a flashing saffron arrow until they reached the abandoned house where he disappeared into the undergrowth.

She'd looked at the house and had the distinct feeling it looked back. It had a forlorn, slightly crazy look about it. Not malevolent, but an air of derangement, like a known lunatic with a blank expression that nevertheless telegraphed unpredictability. She scanned the cracks between the boards on the windows, looking for signs of movement. It didn't look empty. Desolate, yes, but still containing . . . something.

For all of this, the house seemed more real to her than the others. For all she knew they could be fake, neat empty boxes made to look like homes. In comparison to the wild growth here, the other gardens certainly looked, in fact were, by definition utterly fake. Trimmed and snipped, mown and tied back. Controlled. This wounded thing, this was a real house, a real garden. This was the untended truth.

Over time, with regular visits and patience, she had come to understand it. Not to pity it. The house had no use for pity.

*

Before leaving for work this morning John leant against the door frame and watched her hanging clothes on the drier. She knew she was doing it wrong but he didn't intervene, which was so considerate. She didn't appreciate him nearly enough. He'd been doing some research for her. He'd looked up all kinds of information on ways she could begin to correct her thinking with something called *mindfulness*. She couldn't fit the word comfortably into her mind. It made her think of overstuffed beige corduroy sofas being crammed into box rooms.

'It's a good idea to shift your focus away from yourself and try to think more about other people,' he said. There was a silence then he sighed, irked she wasn't really listening to him.

Sometimes it was difficult, her mind wandered, but she did try. She was trying. 'That makes sense,' she said, making eye contact and nodding.

'Something to try,' he said, 'is to do something for someone else every day.'

'Really?' She crossed back into the kitchen. He drained his mug and added it to the collection of crumby plates and glasses gummy with fruit juice. She ran the tap and waited for the water to heat up.

'It doesn't have to be anything big, and you're not to expect thanks for it, or for it even to be noticed. It can be really small, just a little thing you think might make another person's day better in some way. Is my lunch in here?' He shouldered his rucksack. She nodded and put her hands in the soapy water. He ruffled her hair. 'I'll be late tonight,' he said on his way out.

'I'll—'

The door closed behind him. '—leave something for you to reheat,' she said to the empty kitchen. Thinking about what he'd said, it was probably better he didn't hear that. It sounded like she was looking for thanks. Her ego really was a needy creature.

*

The night visits must be managed carefully. Suspecting John would not approve, she waits until he is asleep before slipping out of the house, through the streets to the other side of the estate. It feels almost as if she is entering a fourth dimension, another world altogether, where the air itself is made of different molecules. There are cars in the driveways, sometimes not. They appear and disappear in different locations throughout the week. Recycling boxes appear and disappear on or around collection days. From her daytime detours, when she deposits her supplies of paint and brushes, she knows that the postman delivers. She has seen children coming and going laden with book-bags and gym kits, has heard a dog barking in a back garden. But not once, day or night, has she seen another adult human being coming or going from any of the houses. Certainly not from number twenty-four.

Always returning home before dawn, showering quietly downstairs, she doesn't need to worry about waking John. His medication makes him hard to wake. Even when she slides into bed beside him and feigns sleep, his breathing remains deep and steady. His arm reaches over and rests uncomfortably across her midriff. It's not deliberate, he's still asleep.

She stares at the ceiling and worries about the tall trees behind the house sending out opportunistic ground creepers and ivy, roots snaking underground, working into the foundations, penetrating the water works, undermining the structure. With no one there to save it, the house is dissolving slowly, a bitter pill in the distended mouth of the woodland.

She closes her eyes and attempts the visualisation exercise John told her about. Another of his wellness tips. Or was this the mindfulness thing? She forgets. The point is, to imagine a tiny light in the centre of her chest, and then to imagine it growing and spreading throughout her body and then beyond it, in a steady progression of warmth and clarity. John said she should try then to imagine this same light in someone else, John himself seems the obvious choice, to see this other person filled with golden light and happiness. But her concentration slides and she is thinking of the house again.

*

She props the board back over the inside of the window as best she can and lights the candles, which are all she dares use for illumination, for fear of drawing the attention of passers-by or neighbours. The choice and positioning of the candles is only one variable in the complex equation she is attempting to solve.

There are so many possible shades of yellow. Sunbeam Glow, Honey Pear, Saguaro Blossom, Sparkling Wine, Butter Cream. She is concentrating on the lighter shades, steering well clear of the likes of Goldenrod and Ochre, trying to capture that secret, subtle brilliance she knows the house deserves. No matter how carefully she studies swatches and experiments with tiny sampler pots, the finished effect on an entire wall cannot be predicted. Another coat, even of the same shade, changes everything all over again. She has experimented with stripes and geometric patterns in similar but not identical shades and is now broadening her efforts in a more spontaneous, organic direction. Vines and leaves intertwine and repeat, but with increasing variation. The effect, currently, on the largest wall of the room at the back of the house is almost three-dimensional, at times she feels herself to be within the pattern, moving around inside the yellowness, contained by it, hardly casting a glance back to the room on the other side.

Tonight she is absorbed in the task of adding the right amount of Hidden Sun to precisely the right area. She has to be careful to angle the brush in a particular way with each stroke, incrementally, building up a progression from the centre of the wall out to the edges. The scraping noise of the window board being moved takes a few seconds to break through her concentration and, when she turns, the board is down and John is standing in the place where it should be.

'What are you doing here?' she asks, more curious than anything else. She was sure he'd been asleep when she left but he must have woken and followed her.

'What am I doing here? What the hell are *you* doing here?' He steps over the windowsill and into the room. He is staring at her, shaking his head in angry disbelief at her paint-splattered overalls, the brush in her hand.

What can she say? She finds, with some surprise, that she doesn't feel like saying anything.

He gestures at the empty tins of paint stacked in the corner, the pile of used brushes. The lack of running water means she can't wash them and so she uses a new one every time. She wonders if he will point out her wastefulness.

'How long has this been going on?' He spins in a slow circle, taking in the evolving stages of her vision.

He is certainly surprised. But does he see what she is trying to do? Can he see how much she has given of herself to do it? Quite unexpectedly, like a surprise gift, she finds she doesn't need his approval, cares not a bit for his anger, or his frustration, or any of the other emotions chasing each other around his face. But she would like to know, can he even see it? Can he see her? Does she want him to? She feels herself receding from him, feels the sinuous arms of the pattern on the wall flex and open to admit her.

John's eyes widen. He puts his hand over his mouth and she sees that his face is very pale. She is acclimatised to the paint fumes but they could be overwhelming to him. Or perhaps the shock is aggravating his blood pressure. He turns around and seems to stagger, then folds slowly to the floor and lies there, right up against the side wall. She stands still and lets the reclaimed silence wash around her. He's still breathing. She can see his chest rising and falling. One two three slower four slower five six . . .

But wait.

The brown of John's jacket and the blue of his jeans are dark and wrong against her beautiful yellow. She walks over, crouches down and strokes the brush lightly over his shoulder. He doesn't move although she supposes he will wake up soon. But she has work to do. There is no other option. She will have to paint over him.

Russell Jones

CARTOGRAPHY OF A RURAL LANDSCAPE

the owl makes the tree
the hop makes the frog
the window sets
the widow at her table
she pours the tea
which makes the cup
dries a spill
spies me spying
which makes me

imagine an owl
clasping a branch
a frog
crunched in its beak
the widow
drying the spill
the tree
scratching
at the window

Jeff Kemp

THIS IS BILL FROM BIRMINGHAM

Dear Customer,
I can no longer live without you.

Your PPI
is the reason that I continue.

Your mis-sold insurance
is my passion.

Your loft insulation
makes me ecstatic.

Your needs are a joy,
my every breath is spent
to help your selection.

Press 1 for today's special offer.
Press 2 if you've forgotten,

I'll automatically begin the menu again:
go round in circles inside your head.

And yes, we can get to you
simple as ringing a bell,

and no, you can't stop us:
(we're in sellers' heaven, you're in buyers' hell).

Marcas Mac an Tuairneir

NEÒINEANAN

Cuiridh camhanach an là,
crith air na neòineanan
a dh'fhàsas an lios air
cùl an taighe.

Dùirn bheaga gheala,
dìon nan suain is
gramail fhathast, gun
leigeil an corragan.

—

Fad an là, cuiridh
cuid eòlas air sràidean
a' bhaile seo.

Gearraidh e slighe dhìreach,
a-steach is a-mach às
na clobhsan dorcha is

Fuasglaidh am baile fhèin,
mar ghucan nam flùraichean sin;
blàthaichidh eòlas air mar
dhuilleagan, fàgte fad na sgrìob.

Ach chan fhaigh e suaimhneas
mo liosa ghlais seo.
Chan fhaic e glasadh
neòineanan mo mhaidne.

DAISIES

First-light sends shivers
through the daisies
growing in the glade
behind my house.

Little fists, white and tight
in their slumbers,
still clenched and yet
to unfurl their fingers.

—

This day, some wayfarer
or other will encounter
these time-trodden streets.

He will cut a path,
straight, in and out of
the darkened closes and

The city will itself
unbind like those buds;
experience in bloom,
petals, scattered on his way.

But he will never know the
repose of this little green space.
He will never see my
dawn-daisies breaking.

Pàdraig MacAoidh

GEOGRAPHICAL EXCLUSIONS APPLY

to hear the Gaelic ann an taigh-mòr
air a' chrìch eadar dà shiorrachd
ann an Èirinn far am faighear taic
o gach comhairle gus na dìogan a ghlanadh,
na claisean a chàradh, ged nach robh e
idir gu leòr agus fios gun teagamh sam bith
gun robh an taigh a' grodadh, nach bi
e fada son t-saoghail seo, leis gun robh e –
mar gach taigh-mòr eile – a' tuiteam
às a chèile on mhullach, gun robh
na sglèatan a' crochadh air adhar,
na cabair phreasach nas làine de thuill
na de dh'fhiodh 's it was lovely to hear
the Gaelic aig solas dearg ann an Gleann
Iucha far an do stad car agus shlaighd
fear sios an uinneag agus leig e às –
gu slaodach – cnap cotain a bha stobte
sa bheul ann am beàrn far am b' àbhaist
fiacail a bhith, an cotan air tionndadh
dearg gorm dubh agus air maistrich
le na duilleagan 's an traillich 's an uisge
ronnach ruadh a' ruith sìos a' chlais
sìos dhan it was lovely to hear the Gaelic
anns a' chlò a' chlò a' chlò às am bi
fàileadh m' eilein-sa ag èirigh gach trup
a bhios tu fàs teth agus fliuch aig an aon àm
mar gum b' e comharra feise a bh' ann
rud cho borb bèisteil 's nach urrainn dhut
a chumail ri taobh do chraicinn, nad
achlaisean, eadar do shlèistean, gun iad a bhith
air an suathadh, air an sgròbadh a bhith dearg
's dubh 's geal 's tu ag ràdh eadar fiaclan dùinte

an ceann a chèile Moire Moire Moire it was
lovely to hear the Gaelic aig àm dol fodha
na grèine, gus am bris an là, gu latha-luain,
aig mullach na creige ann an Gippsland
far an do shad an Sgitheanach
Alasdair Mac a' Mhaolain tùsanaich
far an oir an dèidh peilearan
a chur nan casan mar gum b' e plàigh
a bh' annta 's beathaichean leòinte
nach robh fiù 's airidh air tròcair,
nach b' annta ach troc it was lovely
to hear the Gaelic air an t-seann sgeir,
na glasan-làimhe a' bìdeadh d' abhbrannan
's do chaoil-dhùirn agus an t-sàl
a' suathadh d' fheòla agus an reothart
a' lìonadh gun dòchas agad – agus i
an àm a' phreasaidh a-rithist an-còmhnaidh
mar a bha 's mar a bhitheas – ach guth fireann
thar nan tonn a' dùrdail it was lovely

Peter Mackay

GEOGRAPHICAL EXCLUSIONS APPLY

to hear the Gaelic in a big house
on the border between two counties
in Ireland where you could get help
from both councils for cleaning the gutters
repairing the rones, even though it was
never enough and there was no doubt
that the house was rotting, not long
for this world, since it was – like every other
big house – tearing itself apart
from the top down, and the slates
were hanging in air and the corrugating
roofbeams more full of holes than wood
and it was lovely to hear the Gaelic at a red
light in Glencoe where a car stopped and a man
wound down his window and dropped –
gently – a sop of cotton that had been
stoppering a hole in his mouth where once
there'd been a tooth, the cotton now turning
red blue black and swirling chewing
masticating with the leaves and butts
in the red rusted water running down the gutter
towards it was lovely to hear the Gaelic
in the tweed the tweed the tweed from which
the smell of my island rises each time
you get both hot and wet at the same time
as if it was a marker of sex, something so
barbaric and animal you could not keep it
beside your skin, in your armpits, between
your thighs without them being rubbed
and scratched red and black and white
while you say between teeth gritted together
Mary Mary Mary it was lovely to hear

the Gaelic at the setting of the sea, when the day
breaks, till the day of the moon, at the top
of the cliff in Gippsland where the Sgitheanach
Alasdair Mac a' Mhaolain threw aborigines
over the edge, having shot them in the legs
as if they were a plague, or wounded
animals, that weren't worthy of pity
that were nothing but brutes it was lovely
to hear the Gaelic on the ol' tidal rock
the manacles biting into your ankles
and wrists and the brine of the rising
spring tide seasoning your flesh and
no hope left but – it being the time
of the press-gangs again, as usual,
as it was and shall be – a male voice
murmuring over the seas it was lovely

Eilidh McCabe

AMBER

She came in through the cat flap not long after you died and I knew she was you. I was in the living room, stretched out on the sofa, staring up at the plaster flowers on the cornicing overhead. There was a clatter through in the kitchen. Henry had been asleep at my feet all evening, so he wasn't the culprit. He raised his head and swivelled an ear in the direction of the noise.

I thought, 'intruder.' I thought, 'fine, let them rob me.' I thought, 'let them clean the place out.' I thought, 'let them gut me like a fish.' Then I forced myself to my feet, because I was meant to go and look when there was an unexplained sound in my home. I trailed out into the hall and pushed open the kitchen door.

At first I was almost disappointed that I wasn't confronted with a balaclava-clad intruder, knife glinting in the moon-striped darkness. Instead, what stood before me was a mirror-eyed, red-furred thing. Frozen over the upturned bin, face turned towards me. I met her gaze, knowing as I did that it was a her, not just any her, but you. Then as I moved forward, very slowly, socks sliding over the grey linoleum, you moved back towards the door, silent as a glance, and were gone.

From the window, I caught the white tip of your brush fading into the gloom of the hedge. I watched to see if you would return, then headed back through to the living room, where Henry was licking his paw in dainty disinterest. The photos on the mantelpiece smiled at me, flanked by the porcelain shepherdess and the brass carriage clock. I picked up the shot of the three of us at a Christmas market in Vienna. You were holding Julie, like a rugby ball in her thick winter clothes. She looked up at you, a chunk of your terracotta-coloured hair clutched in her little fist, on its way to her mouth. Your yellow-brown eyes met the camera, pupils narrowed to pinpoints in the glare of the flash. It was you in the frame, but it had also been you in the kitchen just minutes before. And it was you in the ground.

*

The next afternoon I was lying in bed when the phone rang. I ignored it. I wanted to make it to dinner time before getting up. But the ringing went on for so long that I became used to it, then worried that it might stop. I stumbled downstairs to answer it. Julie.

'I tried your mobile but it was off,' she said.

'To save the battery.'

'But what's the point in having a phone if it's never on?'

'So I can use it when I need it.'

A pause. 'Okay,' she said, 'it doesn't matter. How are you?'

'I'm grand, love. Adjusting, you know.'

'Good.'

'And you?'

'Yeah, I'm fine.' Another pause. 'I think a bit about her in the coffin. When she didn't look like her.'

'No, she didn't.'

'She wouldn't have worn that, would she?'

'No, I wouldn't have thought so.'

'It's a strange tradition, don't you think? To fill the body with embalming fluid and then have everyone come and look at it.'

I didn't want her to go on. 'Yes.'

'So. When should I come round to sort through the stuff?'

'Her stuff.'

'Yeah.'

I thought about the long day stretched ahead of me with nothing to do and no one to talk to but Henry. 'Today?'

'I can't. But tomorrow.'

'Yes, okay.'

'Are you sure you don't want to come and stay with us? Or for me to stay there?'

I did want it. 'No, Henry and I need our space.'

'Right. See you tomorrow then. Before lunch.'

'Yes.'

'Turn your phone on.'

'I might.'

After I hung up I looked at the wallpaper for a while. It was cream-coloured, textured with raised, soft, spongy stuff that swirled across it like clouds of white midges. I put my fingernail into the centre of one of the soft parts and pushed down. When I removed it a perfect semicircular indentation sliced the surface in two.

I caught sight of a dark form moving outside the window. David from next door was in the driveway, shovelling snow, bundled up in his puffy jacket, scarf and woollen hat with his thick padded gloves that made him look like a lobster. He realised I was looking and waved one of his big fabric claws at me. I waved back. Why was he shovelling my driveway? This had never happened before. Oh, yes. It was because I was old. Old and bereaved. The elderly neighbour who needed everything done for him. He and Emma would have discussed it:

'I'm just going out to shovel the drive, love.'

'Oh, could you do next door's at the same time? He'll not be able to do it himself. And his wife just dead, too.'

'Of course. Poor old soul.'

You're no spring chicken yourself, David, I wanted to say to him. Well into your fifties, at least. I should point it out. But it would be very useful to have a clear driveway.

*

That night I laid a bowl of cat food in front of the back door and shut Henry in the living room so he wouldn't eat it. I went for rabbit flavour; the others were all a bit fishy, and I wasn't sure how foxes felt about fishy things. Then I sat down at the kitchen table with my camera, facing the door, and waited. While I waited, I leafed through your copy of *Tess of the D'Urbervilles* from university, your small neat handwriting all over it. A trail of tiny pieces of yourself, left long before you even knew me.

I don't know how long I sat there, my attention drifting between the printed text and those careful notes, made decades ago, when you were a different person. When you were still a person.

A noise made me look up and there you were, a long ginger thing unfolding yourself through the cat flap. You didn't even wait for your hind legs to come through before you lowered your head and began gobbling the food on the plate. I reached for my camera slowly, very slowly, but not slowly enough, and you looked up and met me with your golden stare. Then you lowered your head again. I lifted the camera: snap, snap, snap. Trapping you. When you'd finished eating, you came forward into the room and started nosing round the bin. I leaned forward and snapped, just as you looked up and departed. But I didn't care. I had got my shot.

*

The next morning I wrapped up warm and stepped out into the bright, cold air. I made my way down my snow-free drive and out towards the high street, where the pharmacy had a one-hour photo development service.

When Julie arrived I was sorting through the photos, laying them out side by side on the table. There was the star shot in the centre: amber eyes meeting the camera head-on. I placed the photo on the mantelpiece next to the one of you in Vienna. The resemblance was uncanny.

I heard her ring and got up to answer the door. She greeted me with a stiff hug.

'How you doing, Dad?'

'I'm well, pet. And you?'

'Bearing up. Got some bits and bobs here left over from yesterday's dinner—' she raised a plastic bag with the faint outline of Tupperware showing through it, 'just in case you won't have time to make yourself anything this evening.'

'Lovely, thanks. I've been eating well though.' In fact I'd had cereal for dinner every night that week.

'That's good. Well, let's go and get this done.'

*

We laid out your clothes on the bed and Julie chose what she wanted. There were a few dresses that would fit her, from before she was born. She folded them carefully and put them aside. I imagined they had been out of fashion for so long they had come back in, and would once again be suitable for a young woman like her.

'Charity shop?' she said, holding up a pair of pristine black heels, and behind her I saw you collapsing onto the bed and kicking them off, rubbing the back of your ankles, saying, 'Last time I try to look smart for work. It's not like anybody notices anyway.'

'Charity shop,' I said, and sat down in the spot where you'd just been.

At some point I realised Julie was crying. I hadn't seen her cry at all, not even at the funeral. She probably didn't feel comfortable crying in front of me. You had always been the one who dealt with that kind of thing. The emotional side. I stood up, walked over and stroked her shoulder, feeling like I was in a country where I didn't know the language.

She was holding a fine silver chain with a bright shard of amber strung on it.

'She wore this all the time,' she said. 'I would hold it while I was falling asleep.'

'Yes, and wrap her hair around your fingers. Necklace in one hand, hair in the other. I'm surprised you remember. You were very small then.'

'I remember more than you might think.'

*

We stopped for lunch and I cooked for the first time in what seemed like an eternity. 'Cooking' was a bit of an exaggeration, though – beans on toast, with cheese grated on top. My culinary skills never were up to much.

When I came through to the living room with the two plates of food, Julie was at the mantelpiece holding the new photo of you.

'This fox came into the house?' she asked.

'Yes,' I said.

'Incredible!' she said. 'Has it come in more than once?'

'Yes. I think Henry's food attracts it.'

'It's beautiful.'

'Yes.'

'Not mangy, like a lot of city foxes.'

'No, it's very well presented.'

'You should be careful with Henry though. They can kill cats.'

Of course you would never kill Henry, because you loved him as much as I did. But I just said, 'Yes.'

*

Later, I ate Julie's leftover pasta standing up in the kitchen, not bothering to reheat it. Plates were piled high in the sink and there was dark grease caked onto the surrounding tiles. How did you clean tiles anyway? Was there special tile-cleaning stuff? Forty years in this house and it had never occurred to me that tiles were a thing that needed to be cleaned. It always just got done.

When I was finished I sat down at the table with the camera, *Tess*, and a pen and pad for taking notes on your notes. I copied down my favourites verbatim, trying to replicate the curve of your letters as closely as possible. 'Hypocrisy!' said one of them, simply, next to an extended chunk of dialogue by Angel. You'd always been that way. Direct.

I must have fallen asleep, because when I woke up you were sniffing at my foot. Instinctively, I reached forward to caress your fur. Before my fingers even connected, your little triangular head flashed forward and snapped at my hand. I pulled back. Too late: the blood was dripping freely onto the floor, and you were gone, the cat flap swinging back and forth in your wake.

I stood up and ran my hand under the tap, watching the pink mixture of blood and water swirl away down the plughole. I closed my eyes and saw you sitting on the edge of the bed not long after Julie was born, your waist still thick, your tummy settling in a flap that came down from your broad hips, snatching the duvet around yourself as soon as you sensed me looking. 'Why do you keep pushing me?' you said.

Under the water, my wound was visible: two clear puncture marks and a row of deep dents between. But as soon as I removed my hand from the stream, the punctures filled up with blood, which overflowed onto my skin and obscured its own source.

*

I woke up in the middle of the night with the bite pounding beneath its plaster. There was ibuprofen under the bathroom sink. I stumbled up to get it, the sudden whiteness of the light when I pulled the string making my eyes ache. Two pills would do the trick. I washed them down with tap water slurped from my cupped hands.

The sun hadn't fully risen when the wound started throbbing again. I brought it close to my face to inspect it in the weak light, peeling back the plaster. The area around it was red and raised, the punctures glistening with a translucent fluid. Definitely infected. I lay still, enjoying the hot rhythm of the pain. Then I turned over towards your side of the bed and the familiar back of your head, speckled white and grey with hair cut short as an animal's fur. I reached out towards it and you flinched away. I closed my eyes and opened them and your hair was long and red, flowing over your pillow and encroaching on mine. You shuffled backwards into my arms, nestling against me so close that if I opened my mouth your hair would fill it.

Again I closed my eyes and then Henry was there, rubbing his stripy face against mine, leaving a faintly fishy trail where his damp nose and the corners of his mouth met my skin.

I pulled him under the covers and pressed him against my chest, but he was restless. He wanted his breakfast. I envied his appetite.

On the kitchen table downstairs was the spread I had laid out for you that time, just the once. A long shot. Toast, cake, three types of jam, blueberries, raspberries, strawberries, yoghurt, honey, orange juice. More food than we could possibly eat. And you, silent in front of your heaped plate, not touching it.

'How can I make you happy?' I asked.

You looked up at me. 'You can be somebody else.'

The food vanished. A set of muddy little footprints was dotted all over the kitchen floor; leading first from the cat flap to the bin, then to the table, then back to the door again.

I brought the pictures through from the living room. With my good hand, I spread them on the table, moved them around. The many sets of amber eyes shifted in front of me. All those times you said you'd leave. And then you did. But now you'd come back more beautiful than ever.

There were many hours to pass before your evening visit. The bite on my hand ached a warning to be careful this time, to be patient. To be different. And I would.

Al McClimens

ODE TO A BURNING ASTRONAUT

The axis tips the planet from the light
as berries unbutton the hawthorn's sleeves
and blackbirds model seasonal colours.
The horse chestnuts are pyromaniacs.
Their fuses fizz, leaves blister in fulminating
displays, dropping in fiery parachute descents
until the park is crazy-paved in embers
while the sky razzle dazzles, its clouds on fire.

In spring I rose before the lark, flew much too high
and scorned the altitude, the sun's hot lick
and thinning oxygen. But the knack of re-entry
eluded my grasp. I burnt my fingers on the cosmic
edge of space. There's no escaping time or gravity.
What goes up as a rocket comes down as a stick.

RELATIONSHIP ADVICE PART THREE:
BREAKING UP IS VERY HARD TO DO

Jist wan wurd, but ah says
the wrang thing. Ah dunno.

Tokn tae you, ah says,
like tokn tae a brick wa'. O,

zat right? she says.
Well, that'll be cheerio

then, she says,
n walks away, slow

like. See ye then, ah says.
Huvnae seen ur since though.

Ma mate, he says
it's a furra best. So,

that's hur telt, he says.
Aye, ah telt ur. But, Jeez-o.

Kevin MacNeil

MAKAR

Buenos Aires, at a vertical distance, as seen from my plane, is vast, teeming and beautiful. Between the airport and the city itself, the sky is such a brilliant blue and the sun so large and golden, the impression you get is of a country that represents its flag. On entering Buenos Aires you are immediately, if happily, lost in one huge, bustling maze. Small wonder that the image we associate most with Argentina's literary genius Borges is a labyrinth.

Odd, that everything here feels appropriate.

As if predestined.

Or perhaps, by virtue of infinity, inevitable.

*

A couple of days later, acclimatised to the pre-winter heat, more or less unjetlagged, I meet Mariana in La Biela café, where we drink coffee and make smiling reference to the pallid statues of Borges and his friend Bioy Casares seated forever at a much-photographed table.

'They look like corpses,' says Mariana.

'Hope it wasn't the coffee that killed them,' I say. 'Anyway,' I add, raising my cup, 'here's to Argentina's living writers.'

As we clink cups I notice Mariana's notebook. Its cover is mesmerising, a gothic pattern of swirls and stars and shadows and buildings and Spanish words and what seem to me expressions without a face. 'That's a hell of a notebook,' I say. 'Those words – what do they mean?'

'It says, "An infinite notebook is a notebook that contains all notes."'

'Where did you get it?'

Mariana pauses. 'There is a man who makes them. But he only makes them for people he knows . . .'

'So I don't suppose I could . . .'

'No, give it a try. Here, I'll write down his address. Don't tell the Book Festival or the British Council you're going into this area.'

*

The following day I leave my watch and other valuables at the hotel and venture through the labyrinth. At long last I come to a dark, narrow alleyway. The door is answered by a thin old man with intense eyes and a dyed-black goatee beard.

He ushers me into a cold dim room that smells of age and leather and ink. I'd expected him to be difficult, somehow, but he speaks good English and tells me he would be delighted to consider making a notebook for me.

Then he stares at me and frowns. 'But what is it for?'

The question flummoxes me. 'Um – writing in. Notes, observations.'

'No!' he says. 'Be specific!'

'For one thing, I want to keep a travel diary.'

'Yes! That's it. A travel diary.' He begins muttering to himself in Spanish.

At length his babble ceases and I ask how much it will be.

'Oh, don't concern yourself with that,' he says, swatting a hand through the stale air. 'We can arrange payment later.'

I thank him and start to leave when a thought occurs. 'When will it be ready?'

'It will be at your hotel reception tomorrow morning.'

'Muchas gracias.'

*

As I retrace my route through the labyrinth, I reflect on what a nice and helpful man he was: a little eccentric, but I adore eccentric people. Still, I have an uneasy feeling. Something about his manner was a little too . . . oily. My chest tightens; I didn't tell him the name of my hotel.

Or did I? I can't remember. I suppose I can always go back to his workshop in a couple of days.

*

But the following morning a telephone call at eight o'clock informs me that a package has arrived at reception. I collect it, and unwrap it in my room. The aroma of leather is strong, nostalgic. The patterns on the cover are similar to, but also different from, the ones on Mariana's notebook. There's even what looks like a map of Scotland.

I turn to the beginning of the notebook to write my name and email address and find with a shock that someone has already done so. Was this meant to be a personal touch? The handwriting is relatively neat, but not decorative: a bit like my own on a good day. How did he know my email address? It feels like an imposition, though, as if a waiter has helped himself to something off your plate on the way to your table.

*

Later that day I plot a route and go for a run through the wider, sunlit streets of the Buenos Aires labyrinth and when I get back to my hotel room buzzing with endorphins and sentences and the heightened sensations of being in a new place I type the following update onto my social media page:

> *10km run through Buenos Aires, done! One of the best ways to get to know a city is to feel its dust under your running shoes. The daydream rhythm helps with writing, too. I love that writers are so much less likely nowadays to conform to the old, sedentary stereotype of being always seated (at desk/pub/café), as though mental and creative wellbeing are not intrinsically related to the physical. (Murakami said, 'Being active every day makes it easier to hear that inner voice.') What did I see on my run? Poverty and wealth, joy and sadness, nature and artifice – bound together, just as they are in Scotland. Miraculous, how travel dovetails cultures and we realise, like the physical and the mental, they were never really separated in the first place, but inter-dependent in this life.*

After a shower I decide to write down some images and ideas in my notebook and my stomach lurches when I turn to the first page and find someone has handwritten my status update verbatim on the first supposedly blank page. My heart contracts. I stare at the words. Is this some kind of game? A cold fever spiders over my skin. I look about the room, mystified. Somehow I feel it's not a prank. I'm reluctant to tell anyone about this lest they think I'm insane. But try as I might to solve the mystery, no solution presents itself. I place the book in the room's safe and sit down to meditate.

*

The next day, I come back from my adventures in the evening and post the following on my social media site:

> So. Today I begun by going for a long run through Buenos Aires, through cool drizzle, then a breeze, then sun. Afterwards I showered and walked off in a seaward direction, on a mission. Buenos Aires is, of course, a port and an islander always gravitates to the sea; if I hadn't seen the sea while here I would have felt like I'd cheated myself. But the place I was really aiming for was Parque de la Memoria, the Park of Remembrance. That glorious sparkling sea is the same sea into which bodies were hurled from planes during Argentina's troubled past. And the Parque de la Memoria honours the memory of those tortured, killed or otherwise 'disappeared' in acts of state-sponsored terrorism. It is a deeply moving place and leaves you with a lasting jolt of horror (of man's inhumanity to man) and gratitude (I am alive, I have been spared thus far, I need to do something worthwhile in this life).

I decide not to open the safe and look at the notebook. But after an hour of agonising prevarication I, inevitably, can no longer help myself. I let the trembling book fall open and of course the words are there on the page, handwritten, dreadful. Fear burns through me like a flu. That night I barely sleep.

*

The following morning I awake groggily and almost before I know what I am doing I pick up the notebook, which I had neglected to put back in the safe. The pages part and reveal a new piece of writing. It doesn't make a lot of sense to me. The piece is only one paragraph long and has a title, *Voice*:

> *A woman with a lovely calm voice goes around the tables*
> *selling sweet delicacies. No one wants them, everyone*
> *buys them – because of her gentle voice. No one who*
> *speaks like this deserves or must ever know evil. Someone*
> *at every table purchases unwanted sweets from her.*
> *Someone at every table falls in love with her – or, rather,*
> *with her voice. As she – or, rather, as her voice – moves*
> *away from each table, it is as if the tiniest of melancholy*
> *sighs takes her place. When she leaves the restaurant*
> *altogether, a form of emptiness descends. The diners all*
> *look around, quietly desolate.*

It makes no sense until I am dining in a nondescript restaurant that evening in the Palermo district and suddenly the door opens, a smiling woman enters and a cold wave of déjà vu runs dizzily through me.

*

That night I cannot sleep. I put the light on and eat the sweets the woman with the sweeter voice sold me. I switch off the light. At length I click the light on again and read Borges until dawn. His thoughts often chime with my own, and I think I know why. For example, in his perfect short story 'The Immortal', Borges wrote: 'We accept reality so readily – perhaps because we sense that nothing is real.' He believed that all writers are the same person, and that person is *no one*. I get out of bed and go to the safe. I press the numerical password into its keypad and the door flicks open. I bring the notebook to bed and think.

I force myself to write in the notebook: *Tomorrow I shall visit the man who made this monstrous book.* Thus resolved, I find it easier to sleep. Who is it who goes to sleep? And where do we go? These are the thoughts drifting inside my head as I myself drift away.

*

Asleep, though not knowing it, I dream a story my Zen teacher once told me. In this story I am observing the monk and then being him.

The monk is at a multi-faith conference. Between lectures he escapes to his room to sit in meditation and say a prayer. While he is doing so, a Christian nun inadvertently barges into his room.

'Oh, I'm sorry!' she exclaims. 'I thought this was my room. I must be next door.'

The monk – who is not yet me – smiles. 'Don't worry.'

The nun is about to turn around when something halts her. 'Forgive me,' she says. 'Aren't you a Buddhist? I thought Buddhists didn't pray? Who are you praying to?'

The monk, who looks like a bald version of me, says: 'No one.'

The nun nods uncertainly and makes to leave. But once again she pauses. 'Forgive me again. But if you're praying to no one, what are you praying for?'

The monk says, 'Nothing.'

The nun gives me, the monk, a look and leaves.

Just as she is opening the door to exit I call out, 'Oh.'

She whirls around: 'Yes?'

I smile. '*There's no one doing the praying either.*'

*

The next morning I wake up with a sense of fulfilment and purpose. I take my shower, coffee and toast slowly so as to enjoy them. I am ready to face the strange man and ask him the questions in my mind. I am happy. Only a country like this could have given birth to a Borges.

I decide to meditate in my room for an hour before following the labyrinth to the notebook-maker's workshop.

*

I sit zazen with a calm intensity. Thoughts arise and pass away; I myself arise and pass away. No such thing as a core of self. No such thing as a fixed unchanging self. People say 'It's all good,' but what they really mean is: 'It's all just as it is.' What, this moment, is missing? Nothing.

Aware suddenly of a presence in the room, I turn. The housekeeper has entered without knocking. She looks familiar. She stares at this foreigner sitting on a meditation cushion in front of a portable Buddha.

Before I can say anything she frowns. 'Forgive me. Are you a Buddhist? I thought Buddhists didn't pray? Who are you praying to?'

For a few long moments I shake my head and then hear myself mouthing: *'There's no one doing the praying either.'*

*

I spend the next few days trying to find my way to the notebook-maker's place. The workshop has disappeared. He himself has vanished.

Only narratives remain.

Kirsten MacQuarrie

MMM

Tosh is not yet awake when I pad downstairs. Pad, my slippered feet scuffing on the floorboards, is as graceful a movement as I can manage these days. My limbs are slow to respond; the bones brittle and awkward like stalks of cane sugar. On the outside, though, my toes have curled. *Frog legs*, I think, whenever I happen to see them.

'*La Grenouille*! How appropriate for the South of France,' Tosh would tease if I told him. But of course, he's not yet awake. Alone, then, my frog feet and I hobble into the living room. There are no curtains: the French, it would seem, have nothing to hide. The sunlight too is different here. It casts long, searching prisms through the window; pure beams of light that illuminate the scene before me in white-hot stripes.

'No depth to it,' I've heard Tosh complain. 'Not like the light in Glasgow.' At home, any sun that reaches us has fought its way through the smoke, the grit, the charcoal clouds of industry. Quarrelsome and sooty: the unmistakable vision of home.

With a sigh, I take my seat and ready myself for this morning's task. The watercolours. Arranged by Tosh's aged yet exacting fingers, the paintings stand in line: floral soldiers, prepared for their passing-out parade. Their colours are delicate, ethereal strokes of violet and rose, yet the linework is strict, almost Japanese in its austerity. Tosh delights in unexpected combinations. We both do.

'Something's missing, something's missing . . .' I heard him grumbling over the flowery troops yesterday: pipe in one hand, paintbrush in the other. 'Would you work your magic on them, dearest?' He flatters me, hooking his arm around my waist (thicker, these days, though he is too polite to say so. Nothing escapes an artist's eye). He winks at me, grinning with the same roguish twinkle that first charmed me back at art school. 'I have only talent,' he whispers. 'You, Margaret, are the genius.' It's not true, of course. No one uses the word 'genius' to describe us now. Certainly not for me, and now not even for Tosh. There were days when he was hailed as an innovator.

An architectural prodigy with European promise, the dynamic young upstart who had the power to elevate his profession literally from the ground up. But those days seem more distant than ever from this side of the Channel. 'Was it the war?' I wonder. Once, our fluency in German indicated sophistication. Travel. Now, it would be treason.

'At least you never change,' I murmur into the paint palette. My fingers creak, but as they warm my hands and I rejoice in the familiar contours of the brush. I will bring these paintings to life, even if I cannot do the same for myself. A moment or two of pleasure in a life that has, I assume, relatively few moments left.

*

'Market time.' Three hours have passed before I speak again. 'I need to buy us something for lunch.' I keep my voice low enough not to wake Tosh fully. Still, I can imagine his grunt of assent. After so many years of marriage, I find that the actual presence of your beloved is not strictly necessary to have a conversation with them. I know what Tosh will say before he does, and so I let him sleep on: sketching him within my mind until his form is conjured before my eyes; moustache and pipe and dry twist of a smile intact.

'How do you find the energy?' my imaginary husband asks me, while the real one snores upstairs. 'How do you find the energy to keep going?'

'You tell me,' I retort. 'I'm your older woman.' Imaginary laughter, from both of us.

Outside in the lane, the prisms of sun have broadened into a glowing midday sweep: a golden wash over the coastline water, bringing it to the boil. I shuffle on my bowed legs towards the fish stall, basket in my hand. I can see, or rather feel, the other wives watching me. They tilt their heads in unison as I pass. Indifferent enough not to seem openly hostile. Too hawkish to be entirely friendly. *Très* French, I decide. But in my heart I know what *elles pensent.*

'She's so old to be so foreign,' they must be thinking. 'What is she doing here?' I have no good answer to give, in either French or English. Head lowered, I pretend to judge the merits of every slice:

buying myself time to calculate what the price of our fish would be
in sterling. I take the long route back. My natural pace, I fear, is more
horse-and-cart than automotive. The women around me travel in
pairs, elbows linked in the sweet sorority of gossip. I hear snippets
of their speech, curt little sentences flicked off their tongues like a
bitter taste. I attempt to translate by brushing the dust from my
girlhood time in Paris.

'Travel?'

'A journey?'

'My greatest journey was to Vienna,' I wish I could contribute. 'I
exhibited my work in Vienna.'

'You mean your husband worked in Vienna?'

'*Non* . . . no.' Even in English, some sentences are lost in
translation.

To my right, a pair of little girls sits on the sea wall. Their legs
dangle over the stonework, thin as school pencils, and I smile when
their socks slide down to their ankles. The girls giggle, plucking
flowerheads from the weeds that grow between the bricks. The
older one removes a petal and plants it, with surprising softness, in
her companion's hair. *Des soeurs avec des fleurs*, I think. Then I think
of Frances.

My sister was always smaller. Smaller in stature as well as in
number: more *petite* even that the younger of these two French waifs
when we were their age. No one believed that a girl like Frances
could grow up to do what she did. No one believed that she could
create those paintings. Those fierce, angular female figures with
minds of their own and limbs that reached out, grappling past
the edges of the paper to take hold of the viewer; seizing him by
his lapels and shaking him into the new century. She created each
one, and she created their frames too. Beat, press, compel: day after
day she manipulated sheets of pure metal into the elegant submission
she craved. Journalists often remarked on those frames, writing
about us in their art magazines and circulars. 'The Marvellous Miss
Macdonalds', I believe one of them called us.

We wore flowers in our hair too, in those days. With sudden
clarity, vivid and more startling than the French sun at its worst, I

can recall Frances and I painting side by side. What year could that have been? What was she working on? In the heat of the memory I am transfixed by my own canvas: trellised with paintwork in lilac and green, and bejewelled with stone beads I set straight into the mix. My largest artwork yet. I remember its composition: three blocks of board fixed together until the span stretched wider than my arms. *The May Queen*. One of my finest. Tosh made a companion piece, his own complementary version, but that came a little later. For now, it was Frances at my side. She played with my tools, laughing as she wove the beads and flowers into her hair. Both of us were redheads, then, but hers was the darker hue. A glinting garnet auburn, framed by a garland of flora. A Celtic vision of Millais's *Ophelia*.

'You're the May Queen,' I said.

'May Fly, more like,' Frances shot back. 'I live for my art, but I live only one day.' She closed her eyes; hung her head to one side. Playing dead.

1899. The year was 1899. The year both of us became engaged. Does a woman ever burn more brightly than the time of her engagement? Chosen, not yet frozen: the hope of a brush poised before a blank canvas. I hear that Herbert destroyed most of her work. He destroyed most of her. 'Mrs Herbert McNair,' the obituary began. 'Wife and mother, and a quite lovely amateur watercolourist.' It was only after reading that my tears began to fall.

Tosh is awake when I return. A little breathless, but chirpy in his mood; somehow he always manages to wheeze with a Scottish accent. I catch him peering through the curtainless window across the bay, scrutinising the outline of the rocks at the cove. He has painted them before. Will he do so again? Behind his glasses, I see him frown. Lines that do not release. I shuffle towards him and we embrace, the meagre basket of fish askew between us.

'The watercolours look wonderful, my dear,' he compliments me. 'I hope you don't mind that I went ahead . . . ?' One hand still holding mine, the other gestures to a signature freshly inked onto the nearest painting. CRM/MMM. 'So the world will know we made them together.'

'Will they sell?' I want to ask.

'I don't know,' he does not want to answer. Instead, he says:

'I'm tired, Margaret.'

'Tired of here? Of France?'

'Tired.'

As *le soleil* finally simmers down to its embers, I dare to open our correspondence. Bills, predominately. A great number of bills. Plus the odd salutation: we still have many acquaintances, if few true friends left. I shove the remaining bundle back into their drawer and attempt to close it. Something snags. I groan, the tone sagging like a bellow, and reach in to remove the problem. Our passports. I lay them out on the table. We may need them again soon. The covering envelope is annotated with fat, amateurish calligraphy; the blottish handiwork of an overeager desk clerk. **Mrs Charles Rennie Mackintosh.** I stretch for my brush. Paint over. Bring to life. **Margaret Macdonald Mackintosh.**

I hear a cough behind me as Tosh moves to return upstairs. My head makes a half-turn of its own accord: a wife's instinct to check that he has recaptured his breath. The movement places a vase of flowers in my sightline. The real-life models of what we labour to depict. Already, some have started to wilt.

'Too Scottish for the French heat?' I ask one. The sallow corners of its petal crumble at my fingertips. Gently, with the touch I usually save for art, I cradle what remains. Place it behind my ear. And I am the May Queen for a moment; a flower soon forgotten.

Iain MacRath

ISOPODUM (SGLEATAIR)

creutair cruthaicht'
mus do shiubhail facal
tarsainn bile
gluasad gu slaodach
tarsainn chairt Valentine
leagt' ann an cabhaig
tarsainn làmh-sgrìobhaidh
a tha crìonadh

Iain Macrae

ISOPODUM (SLATER)

creature created
before word travelled
across lip
moves slowly
across a Valentine
knocked over in haste
across handwriting
which is fading

METEOR

Gualainn a' priobadh ort,
casan togail oir-dhust bhon bhlaes
le siofal lannaireach.
Planaid ceangailte ri brog
– Jim Baxter a mheit –
An e èibhleag a tha sin na bheul?
Suathadh tarsainn na cruinne is mach à seo e
's cha bheireadh sgoilear
neo rocaid na gealaich fhèin air.

Nuair a thachair mi ris mu dheireadh
bha e a' cromadh bhon bhus,
gualainn suas ri chluasan,
làmhan nan crith,
feuchainn ri 'n gnothach fhaighinn air roll-up.
Bhrògan brist' a' dèanamh siofal slaodach
's iad còmhdaicht' le luaithre.

METEOR

Shoulder winks at you,
feet raise gold-dust from blaes
with a glittering shuffle.
Planet tied to boot
– Jim Baxter mate –
Is that an ember in his mouth?
A sweep across the globe and away
and neither scholar
nor moon rocket will catch him

When last I met him
he was stooping from the bus,
shoulders up to his ears,
hands all trembling,
trying to control a roll-up.
Broken shoes making a slow shuffle
and all covered in ashes.

TIODHLAC

Air an fheur bhrùite
tiùrr, tiodhlac de dh' itean
liath-ghlas, liath-gheal.
Lorgan de dh' orains.

Tha sacramaid fala
criathraicht' tro ghob-fhiacail
is amhaich bhog bhàthte
air sìoladh dhan talamh dhorch.

Os ar cionn, air sglèatan
liath-ghlas, liath-dhubh,
tha coitheanal suimeil a' draghadh
an casan ann am faire shàmhach.

PYRE

On the bruised grass
a pyre of feathers
blue-grey, blue-white.
A trace of orange.

A sacrament of blood
sieved through beak-teeth
and downy drowning neck
has seeped into the dark soil.

Above, on the roof slates
of blue-grey, blue-black,
a respectful gathering
shuffles in silent vigil.

Ian Madden

CRACKS IN AN EDIFICE OF SHEER REASON

Wind-up gramophone within reach, notepad in my lap, I'm sitting in the shade of the oldest of the oaks and keeping watch over the hedge in the corner of my garden. After nearly half a century they are before my eyes again: the pictures my father painted of gossamer-winged figures hovering high above Montrose Royal Lunatic Asylum.

He filled dozens of sketchbooks while there. He was especially fond of guardian angels. He saw them everywhere. They were what he drew most often. The poor fellow never stopped hoping the fulsome hope that his 'volumes of ideas' might somehow make money for his family.

*

Among my post this morning, a polite, civil, demented letter (by no means the first) from a woman writing in the hope of being appointed you-know-who's housekeeper. I was at a loss. If she could find out where I live, you'd have thought she'd have the mother wit to work out the rest.

*

My neighbour's little girl sometimes joins me on these afternoon vigils. For a five-year-old she can keep very still – and for fairly long periods. She does not doubt the fairies but, on her last visit, she did express a momentary doubt as to my nationality.

*

I'm not very well up on the lunacy laws of Scotland. Maybe they have changed since my father's incarceration. There is such distance now, in miles and time. It all seems to belong to another century. Which, of course, it does.

Do Scottish asylums still boast of their 'trout fishing' and, more worryingly, their 'good shooting'?

Strong as she was, the Mammy claimed she could not cope with her husband. She had him consigned to the Home for Inebriates at Drumlithie: the first of his dreadful other homes. Not long afterwards he drew his first fairy tree.

*

I'm aware what people think. According to a recent *Punch* cartoon it is I who am the grotesque, the caricature; not the svelte ruminating Englishman from whose pipe-smoke a bumbling old Scottish duffer has materialised.

Still, it would be wrong to say I don't quietly relish the consternation I've caused among the keepers of reason.

*

Writing stories – nothing more than lying persuasively, after all – calls for stealth. Like life itself.

And stealth was what I had. At Southsea I'd wait until after hours before sneaking out to polish the plaque by the front door. That way no one would know the eye doctor couldn't afford domestic help. On the walls of my consulting room I'd hung a number of watercolours, several of which were painted by my father. In the mornings, waiting for patients who never came, I alleviated the boredom by jotting down ideas for fictions. Joseph Bell returned to my mind. His character was the story I wanted to tell, the occurrences I came up with were very much secondary. When the first adventure finally saw the light of publication, someone complimented me in print on my knowledge of London. Of course one accepts praise. It's always gratifying. No need to venture anything as deflating as the truth: when I thought up the tale in question I'd been in England's capital precisely twice in my life, and both times very briefly. I wrote the piece while living at an extremity of Hampshire, with a map of the London streets open in front of me. Surprising how easy it is to be taken for an expert without even trying.

*

My parents' lodger was a man I never took to. Firstly, it was never answered why Dr Waller needed to be anyone's lodger. He was well enough off. He could trace his lineage (and presumably his wealth) back into the mists of time. Agincourt was mentioned. The Mammy fell under his spell. 'Spell' being the only word for it. I was away from home for the greater part of my schooldays; however, when I was sixteen or so this man coached me for the entrance exam for medical school. He might, I now see, have exercised an influence over me in that one regard. I wasn't the only one he influenced.

*

In six months the decade will be over. The 1920s have flown by. With each passing year the calendar becomes less and less relevant; nothing more than a knick-knack. Things other than dates leave their impression, sometimes quite literally. In Egypt in 1895 a horse kicked me in the face. I'm lucky to have a right eye. My right eyelid has drooped ever since. Not all our souvenirs are physical. There are similar assaults on our mental and spiritual attributes, though the evidence left by these onslaughts isn't always visible.

*

The protagonist in the stories I dreamed up while waiting for patients on those mornings in Southsea (in my recollection it is always Tuesday and always drizzling with rain) was a way of passing the time and, importantly, of earning money. In short, they were what I resorted to when the good people of the town who had ophthalmic concerns saw fit to consult someone else.

The devotees of these tales always took me aback rather. They still do. It remains perplexing, the hole in their lives that my creation seems to be stopping up. Now that a space in my life (or my life itself) is being filled with something other than what they are used to and what they condone, they, the self-appointed keepers of reason, are inclined to attack.

Readers can be very unforgiving when a writer doesn't stay where they've shelved him. They are intent upon stranding me on an atoll of their own devising. I shall resist. I do resist. If ridicule is the price I have to pay then pay it I shall. Pay it I do.

*

As she joined me the other day in my garden, the little girl from the house nearby asked me what 'couthie' meant. I had to own that I did not know.

'I thought you were from Scotland,' she accused.

'I am.'

'Well, it's a word from Scotland.'

And she looked at me, examining not so much the droop of my right eyelid as the sudden and very suspicious shortfall in my Scottishness.

*

The Mammy became her lodger's lodger. Dr Waller took the two middle floors of a house in the most aristocratic square in Edinburgh. No one who could afford to live there – then or now – need take in lodgers. If this situation were to be used in fiction, it would have to be nudged, topped and tailed, or just rewritten. In a story it would make sense, I suppose, to have the character based on the Mammy move to the new address with the character based on Waller only after the character based on her husband was safely out of the picture. But my mother *and* my father went to lodge with their sometime lodger. A fact like that breaches the demands of fiction.

Perhaps those civilised surroundings were where my father's removal was, if not plotted, then certainly suggested: brought up by the helpful doctor as a possibility: something to bear in mind.

*

When I was in my early twenties Uncle Dicky stood me lunch at the Athenaeum. Over the meal he tried to persuade me to remain a Catholic. I insisted to the whole family that I would not subscribe to any philosophy that could not be proved. That was the zenith of my Reason Period. A version of what I said to Uncle Dicky then is being said back to me now, and with just as much conviction. In those days, 1883 or thereabouts, I was Bell's avid disciple, charging and indestructible. What I had yet to tackle – or what had yet to tackle me, the strapping rugby player – was loss.

This summer, as the biblically allotted span approaches, I can say I've had my fair share of being tackled. I see fragility everywhere; not least where I used to see armour-plating.

*

When I'd had more than enough of my creation, I tried to escape him by the only means I knew. Not even that worked. What I had hoped would be the end of him proved to be just a bend in the road. I was offered more money than I could refuse to resurrect him. Still, if a devotee can believe in (I almost wrote 'swallow') the Reichenbach Falls, you'd think spiritualism – or fairy-spotting – wouldn't be such a leap of faith.

Apparently not.

*

Breaking open the children's boxes and, when there was no alcohol to be had, drinking furniture polish.

This was only some of what my mother claimed her husband had done. Anyone who could stoop to such things would be better out of the way. Neither my brother nor my sister ever spoke about why their mother's husband had been taken away and locked up. However, at this moment in this peaceful garden, the terrible reasons ventured in those far-off days seem unbelievable.

Across this distance, I want to know more. I am curious now as I wasn't then. There is no one left to ask.

*

The lawn has a just-mown aroma. The flowers are at their liveliest. While watching for movement among the hedges and the flowerbeds, who should come to mind but Edward Elgar's wife; a devoted soul called Alice. She had a quiet way of speaking and of lightly touching your arm as she confided.

I really must rouse myself and get that gramophone going. I'll never entice them at this rate.

*

After his confinement the occasions my father came up in conversation were few and far between. Awkward euphemisms were mentions of a sort. But even they stopped. The Mammy, if she spoke of him, always did so from the standpoint of victim; but a victim who, it has to be said, had the upper hand.

The Mammy did not marry the wrong man. She married a docile man, a dreamy man, a kindly man not going fast enough for her – or in the right direction. Divorce was out of the question. One thing strikes me about my mother's account of her marriage, something I did not doubt at the time. But which now conjures a situation impossible to credit. That is, a domestic circumstance in which she wasn't the boss.

*

The other day I submitted to an interview – a mistake. As always, the newspaperman came equipped with his story and merely watched me for signs of it. The devotional spire formed by his respectful fingertips as they touched under his chin prepared him, so it seemed, to receive wisdom. He chose his words with exaggerated care. I did my utmost to be unvenerable but he wasn't having that. His estimation of what he took to be my understated and surely cunning rationality might well have been restricting the flow of blood to his brain. Despite my best endeavours to put him at his ease, he persisted. He was determined to find me an exemplar. Though of what, I didn't care to think.

*

I never went to visit my father. Not once. His loss of reason embarrassed me. When he died, I felt relief. He got an obituary in the newspaper. It mentioned his young son the doctor and writer; the son (the account did not say) who never went near during the years of his father's confinement. Of all the needles memory jabs at me, this is the sharpest, the hottest, the most shaming. I was always busy. There was always something else – something better – to do. Prior engagements rained down on me. And just think how the

Mammy would've taken it had I made so bold as to visit the man she had so consummately rid herself of.

*

The silence in my garden is detailed, nuanced.

To be suspended in the fluid of derision is, to me, a more comfortable state than that of lionisation. I have learned to make it so. I haven't reread any of my stories about you-know-who since they were written. There's been too much to write without that. If an aficionado chooses to read a tale then read it again – from this angle and that, prodding it with a finger, stabbing it with a scalpel – and thereby inspect the life out of it, good luck to him. I was and am determined to keep moving.

For some, logic is the be-all and end-all. The rationally minded will not brook what are, to them, unsatisfactory reasons or not reasons at all. The Swiss say of find-faults: 'He sees only the holes, not the cheese.'

Admirers are merely detractors-in-waiting.

*

When I saw the envelope, when I read its enclosure, I had my doubts. Had the accolade been bestowed in recognition of the writings of which I was then most proud – my reports from the South African War – I should not have hesitated. My mother, however, had no such reservations. She insisted I must accept. Doing so would be 'one in the eye' for those who looked down on our family for its Irish ancestry. I'd never contradicted the Mammy in my life and was not about to start at the age of forty, or was it forty-one? So I became a knight of the realm for, it seemed to me at the time, no better reason than helping my mother get one over on those she saw as her foes.

*

I made it my business to find out what 'couthie' means. Should the child call by I shall tell her. It will be a little belated and I fear will not be entirely satisfactory at this remove, but I have the meaning to hand.

*

It is clear to me now in the shadow of this tree, decades and worlds away, that my father did not lack reason; he possessed reason of a different kind merely.

Weak he may have been; feckless he most certainly was. He was not, however, a thief and was never violent. Did he steal from his own children's boxes? Would he have dared raise a hand to his formidable wife? His children were not frightened of him. Though they became frightened of what happened to him, of where he was taken, and of what it was he was said to be.

*

I have developed the habit, when alone, of pressing my knuckles to my lower lip then gently breathing in. On the back of my hand I can smell the soap I used when bathing this morning. Sometimes there's another smell. This one is not so distinct. It is a compound of greengages, gunfire smoke and the enteric fever ward. At other times, though this may be a little fanciful, it is my own death I can smell. Corporeal death, I mean. Happily, from time to time, the stern, clean, capable smell of the Mammy will return. Today, though, the smells are those of a garden in high summer and the warm casing of the gramophone.

*

Alice Elgar – her fingers gently and, it would seem, daringly on my forearm – told me about the morning her husband received 'the letter'. At first he had suspected it was the work of a malicious prankster. Checks were made. He was assured the offer was genuine. Still he dithered. What made up his mind was a simple comment made by the erstwhile Alice. I remember her confidential tone as she recalled what she had told her famous but vacillating husband, 'That'll show them.'

It made me wonder then (and still makes me wonder) how many people accept an honour viewing it as did the Mammy and Mrs Elgar: a gesture which, in a certain light, is as rude as it is regal. If indeed it does amount to a riposte, it is one which 'Sir' doesn't have to expend time or dignity making on his own behalf.

*

It looks like the little girl won't be joining me today. So it's just me and – in a moment – the tunes on the gramophone records.

There is shadow here, though hardly any breeze; I smile, realising that the spectral wraiths my father drew while incarcerated are not too unlike the guests I am certain to entertain if I am vigilant enough, and welcoming.

My belief in the recent fairy pictures – photographs! – have caused those still captive to reason to think I've lost mine. Retired rationalist that I am, I am more concerned with the importance of belief, not the quality of it, nor how much it will stand up to inspection and dissection. If the hopes on which I insist – of the spirit continuing after death and of spotting fairy folk in my garden – create cracks in an edifice of sheer reason, then so be it.

Let the structure split. Let it crumble. Let it fall.

Who's to say there's no sense to be had among the ruins?

It's comforting to think that over the course of a lifetime beliefs possess a symmetry we can only partly adduce. The rest is stumbling. The rest is waiting, anticipation and repose. And there's no repose greater than that of not having to prove anything any more.

I crank the portable gramophone. The music is a plodding romp, this side of jolly. The fairies may appear. Or they may not. Either way, with sufficient fortitude and patience, waiting in the expectation of consolation can itself be very consoling.

86

Susan Mansfield

EIGHT REASONS

'Build your cities on the slopes of Vesuvius!'
—Nietzsche

Because one day all this will pass away.

Because geothermal energy is a completely sustainable and
    environmentally friendly way to heat your home.

Because it doesn't matter if the architecture goes out of date.

Because the trace elements in the soil, left behind by past lava
    flows, will do wonders for the allotment.

Because, sometimes, extinct really does mean extinct.

Because the kind of people who prioritise income from
    long-term capital investment funds will leave you
    well alone.

Because everyone else is kidding themselves.

Because of the view.

SLOTH

'The old do not walk more slowly because they have plenty of time.'
—Roger McGough

I am not slow as some
understand slowness; the world
too quickly mistakes tardiness
for taking time to give the matter
appropriate thought. Travel
deliberately, place each foot
with care; the upside-down
tightrope-walker gets there
just the same. Agility is not
speed, it is continuous motion,
each stubby limb holding within it
the possibility of flow; one can
hang by a single toe if one attends
to balance, and oh! the view.
The wise have learned not to
rush out to greet the inevitable;
a somersault is no less
precarious when performed
in slow motion. Above all,
the trick is not to surprise
the universe; better to fold
the fabric of time around oneself,
allow matter to flow back, like honey,
into the space one has left.

Lynsey May

SCARS ON THEIR KNUCKLES

We are hoping for a visit from Alexander this weekend, the first in several years. I've bought in extra food and turned down a bed. He has promised to come and broken that promise more times than I would like to admit. I don't blame him.

Brian will be relieved if Alexander cancels, but will pretend to share my disappointment. I know that deep down, he would like me to struggle more – to find the fact of Alexander as difficult as he does. But I remember when my boy was still so small and flexible that I could scoop him up in my arms and squeeze tight. I long to return to that time. I yearn for it so strongly that I sometimes sleep with my back to Brian, a toddler-sized pillow hugged to my chest instead. I want few things more than this visit from my son, even if he no longer fits into the space I made for him. The last time we saw each other, he had to lean down to give me a hug.

Even then, long after the end of the bad times, I got the feeling that he had grown – changed – too much. He held me and my welcomes and my words could get no higher than his shoulders, where they dribbled uselessly down his back. He will be no shorter, but I can't help hoping that things will be better now.

I'm making a loaf of bread. It costs more to bake one than it does to buy, but once I'd thought of it, I couldn't get the idea out of my head. I leave the dough to rise as I start working through our little pile of washing and soon the smell of warming yeast begins to tickle my nose and coax hungry growls from my stomach. I could not eat a bite, but the smell takes me back and I suppose this is what I wanted. It was never my mother who baked, my memories are all of my grandmother, but it's the same feeling.

*

I have only seen Alexander twice since he was relocated. There are friends of ours who have not faced their children yet, who have cut them out of their lives almost completely, but you can see the edges that have been left behind. No scalpel-sharp incisions, instead great long rents that heal slowly and painfully.

Brian didn't manage to come with me the last time I met Alexander. He wanted to see his son again, I know he did, but when the morning arrived he locked himself in the bathroom. I called to him through the old green door and he couldn't tell me why he was in there, only that he couldn't bring himself to come out.

I left without him. Off to the chain café we'd agreed to meet in. One of the few places where, in those early days of recovery, the old and young guards could meet without raised eyebrows or eaves-dropping. They know how to create a false sense of comfort in places like that; happy elderly Italians on the wall with faces curled in smiles and pretzel-brown hands clasped. Alexander was skinny and there were lines under his eyes. He didn't ask me where his father was and, although I had already forgiven him, forgiven him again and again, I felt yet another layer scraped from my heart.

*

When he was a child, I'd believed Alexander was capable of anything. I'd known him to be unique, exceptional, but I also understood I was not alone in that. Don't all parents dote on their children? Afterwards, lots of people started hunting their memories for warning signs and claimed they'd seen it coming. A dark shape on the horizon, a tremor under their feet. I don't know why they wanted to think that. I'm far happier certain that I never suspected, that what happened to Alexander and so many of the other teenagers wasn't recognisable. Certainly wasn't preventable. If it was, how could we live with our failure to prevent it? We'd seen what we wanted to.

Not all of the teenagers took part, but it was a huge majority. So many that I can stand in any one of the big shops on the high street and reach out and touch one. One of those young men or women who looks just like anyone else now. Who not so long ago would have exploded at the touch of my hand. If I was lucky, they might have only spit in my face. If they were one of the hardliners, I might have come away bleeding or broken. So empty, the young people were then. Soulless children. And here they are again now, buying bottles of fizzy juice or boxes of eggs, so conscious of their place in the world and mine, and desperate to pretend that things are as they were before.

We try not to fault them now. We are trying to heal and we'll do it any way that we can. I've read many of the news reports claiming that it was not the teenagers themselves who organised the horrors, that there was a mastermind behind it. They say ideas spread in the lower reaches of the internet, in the careful altering of memes and messages that looked innocent to most of us mere 'tech-competents', but which held a level of meaning few of us understand even now.

I have watched the professors and the researchers on the TV, in their smart suits or defiantly casual t-shirts and jeans, but many of us remain unconvinced when it comes to grand claims of orchestration. One man was arrested not long afterwards but was released when the news sites were flooded with video and written evidence exonerating him. Maybe there was a composer and I am wrong, I don't see how it would make any of the last few years easier to bear.

Alexander and I have never spoken of the lost months. All I can do is remember the quiet in his room, the gentle tapping of his fingers on the keyboards, the smile I saw slowly recede. I thought it was only the normal distancing of growing up, I had no idea what he was becoming.

The real change, when it came, was not a gradual process. In one day, our angry and disenfranchised teenagers disappeared and were replaced by strangers. They had no eyes, no empathy. They hated us. Had been learning to hate us for a long time and, despite everything they did, it took a long time for us to learn to hate them back. And now, we try to stop.

Reports around the world show footage of our riots and offer analysis. None can capture quite how terrifying it was to know our own children were the ones who wanted to see us overthrown. Removed. They were clever about it though, the teenagers created their own exchanges and travelled to ensure they were dealing not with their own parents. Instead, they dealt with ones they could more easily imagine to be the enemy.

Those were months of terror. An aged man was kicked to death just a few streets away. I saw our lollipop lady forced to stand in the street with no top on, her old breasts puckered in the cold. As quickly as the nightmare had begun, it ended. One summer of many, one that will remain singular.

The police regained control, the teenagers fizzled out, they were seen sleeping at the side of the road. Ragged and hungry, blood obvious under the grime on their hands. Brian and I, we had a better run of it than most and still I've been having the panic attacks and he has started napping half of the day away. Our world was fractured, and it has not returned to the way it was. No matter how much I wish it.

We thought, all of us olders, that the UK would not be able to continue after the explosion of rage, but it does. The country acclimatised and when they took off their masks, the teenagers were revealed to be as confused and panicked as we were. We'd known things were bad for them, but things were bad for us all. We'd assumed they knew we were all in the mess together. Things are worse now, of course, but some of us need to understand what they were looking for. We have to.

Alexander is more than half an hour late. Brian is measuring and cutting pieces of wood. I wish he wouldn't, but I won't stop him. I'll only hope that when Alexander comes, Brian will put down the saw and join us. I keep away from the windows. I don't want to know who might be watching our son approach. There's nothing any of them could say to change how I feel about my son, but their judgement is still painful.

*

As I contemplate my cooling loaf, picturing the way it would land solidly in the bin, the knock at the door finally comes.

In his hand is a plastic bag with biscuits from the shop he works in. He told me the last time he would apply for college as soon as he'd completed his probation. I hope he'll be able to tell me he's done it. There are a lot of things I wish he could tell me, but if he is able to stand straight and let me whisper into the bones that shield his heart, maybe I could find yet another way to forgive without him saying a word. He reaches out to hug me but our closeness is not as it should be and in an instant we are apart again.

I usher him in. He smiles and hands me the biscuits. I lead him through to the kitchen and offer a cup of tea. As I make it, we listen to the sound of the saw in the other room. Brian must know his boy is here. Once, I could have shouted through or sent Alexander to fetch him. Now, extra care is needed. Hope is needed. It beats inside me but I can't tell whether Alexander has managed to hang on to any at all.

I give my son his cup of tea and look at his hand as it brushes mine. It is a reminder of all we've lost. Alexander has never told us what he did or didn't do during the riots. We know it must have been bad. He would have been back sooner if it wasn't. He grips the hot cup and as the skin of his hands tightens, I have to look away.

I won't walk to the door to call Brian, although I want my husband to be the man I once thought him. More so, I want my son to be the one we deserved. Most of all, I want Alexander to have the life we hoped for him. Even now, I don't see how he can. There are scars between his knuckles and lines scrawled below his eyes and there's nothing I can do or say to take them away.

Donald S. Murray

HOW THE LOCH NESS MONSTER STOLE MY HUSBAND

He had been for decades on her trail,
determining the drop-zones where she dived, her size and scale,
the encumbrance of her head, the length of tail,

and there were times he stepped into our bedroom
wearing her scent – a faint, unfathomable perfume –
and hummed the song he said was the mating tune

that must have drawn him one dark night
not far from Arbriachan when she swirled towards his side
and pulled him close against her – neat, spiralling and tight,

how she must have coiled against another of her kind
centuries before that. Oh, I know they'll never find
him. It'll be a case of out of sight, out of mind

in a different way from how my sister claims
I'm long out of mine. They'll argue that he never came
home one night, our life on Millburn Road too tame

for him, that he preferred the thrash and thrust of another's
              limbs,
a different kind of current, rhythm
than those murky depths I know he slipped within.

Julie Rea

SHARK TOOTH

It's the THUD THUD THUD on the front door at two in the morning that makes you jump out of bed. The polis barge in and drag your brother from his room, he's in his boxers, arms cuffed behind his back. And your heart feels like a grenade, and you're screaming, and so is your ma, and your da is comatose in the bedroom. Your ma grabs the arm of the polis, but he swats her away and she stumbles. Whit's he done? she shrieks, and they say he was thieving, and his lip is burst, teeth the colour of ripe plums. You hear the smack of the baton as it whacks his jaw, and your ma swears he was here all night, and he was, this time he really was. But they're piled on top of him now, all you see are the dirty soles of his feet; his ribs sound like knuckles being cracked.

And your ma keeps you off school the next day. You fill a basin with hot water and a squirt of Fairy Liquid, rip up old dusters and wash the blood off the walls. It doesn't really clean it, just streaks and smears it. Your ma chucks the duster, gets the Benson & Hedges from her overall pocket and sparks up. My boy, she moans, glaring at his blood, look what they fuckin' pigs done to my boy. And you rinse the cloth in the basin, biting down hard on your bottom lip; the water has clots and pieces of skin floating in it. That's bits of my brother in there, you think, a cattle-prod shock to your skull. His tooth is buried somewhere in the shag-pile carpet. Each day is a plastic bag being pulled down further over your face.

*

It's lying up on the couch, watching *Pebble Mill at One*, hot-water bottle over your belly, 'cause you're on the blob and the cramps are killing you. Your ma smacks her slipper aff the back of your head and says, Looks like I'll go and get my ain fuckin' fags then? And you think, Aye you could dae wi' the exercise ya fat cow, but you don't say it. She slams the door shut, and you watch *Neighbours* and decide that when you grow up you're going to get a perm, and live in Australia, and definitely shag Jason Donovan. Later, you hear the key in the lock, your ma shuffling and wheezing along the hall, and she forgot the milk, so it'll be dry Weetabix again for breakfast.

*

It's sitting up the back of the class with the dafties, ripping pages from textbooks to make paper aeroplanes, and your teacher looks at you the same way folk look when they see bird shit on their windscreen. He clears his throat, and says I'll try that again, shall I? And he opens the book, reads a poem, and you pretend not to listen, but the words lick around your brain; and it sounds like you're dreaming, and it sounds like grace, and you feel like you've swallowed a stone, because it's hard to hear there's beautiful things in this world.

And you stare at the leather patch on the elbow of his tweed jacket, glancing at his mouth – crooked front teeth and ginger stubble – the poem forming a shape in mid-air. The janny is mopping the corridor outside and the stench, lemon vinegar, shoots up your nose just as the teacher says the word '*surfacing*'. You roll it around silently in your mind.

Surfacing.

And you walk home from school, bag slung low over your shoulder, with your best mate Izzy, who smells like Vosene and Dewberry from the Body Shop. She only managed to sneak one of her ma's cigs, so you go twosies on it. She's talking about a lad in fifth year she gave a blowjob to, but you don't believe her, 'cause her ma belted her jaw when she saw her just talking to some ned at the school gates. But you're not really listening anyway, that poem is lodged in your head, like a razor stuck in a peach. You walk through the forest beside the burn, and Izzy takes the last drag, before flicking the butt into the water. The sky is bright blue, but the trees smell stale, like the inside of fusty cupboards, and you wish you'd brought gloves 'cause the tips of your fingers are numb. When you get home, you lie on top of your bed and, with your tongue, trace words from the poem on the roof of your mouth.

*

It's lugging the artificial Christmas tree from out the airing cupboard, hanging plastic baubles on the branches, then propping it up on the sideboard, 'cause if you placed it on the floor it wouldnae even come up to your knees. Your da, slumped low in his chair and still wearing his leather jacket, 'cause he forgot the bookies was shut, gets weepy for the Queen's speech. What a wummin, he says, chucking his empty can into the fireplace. You wrote your brother a card, but you don't know the address of the jail, so you just put it under his pillow. Your ma wears sunglasses in winter, and it's no 'cause she's going on a skiing trip, it's to hide the fuck-off bruises underneath. In a week, says your ma, it's a new year, a brand-new year, but she's saying it like, the chemo isnae working, the cancer's spreading. The cancer is spreading.

*

It's sitting up the park, on grass that's damp from snow turned to slush, sharing a bottle of cider that you got from the Spar. And it's pitch black, and you can only see fuzzy outlines, of see-saws and swings, and guys you don't know. You hear Izzy in the distance, but you're not sure if she screamed, or just laughed. A jagged patch of inky sky above the trees: the stars look like grey fillings, and the air has claws in it. You keep swigging from the bottle of Strongbow, and everything loosens, and it feels good to fall.

And somebody is groping under your jumper, he smells like roll-ups and cheap aftershave, and he's trying to yank your bra to one side. It's only a 32A, you think, so why fucking bother? A hum of fear makes you shiver, bile starts to rise from your belly, and you spew up on the grass. The place is spinning, spinning, hot steam rising from the puke, throat burning, and you remember a piece from the poem—

> *pale limbs slicing through a green lake,*
> *grey dress circling gaunt as a shark;*
> *sinking, the water burns into her bones,*
> *surfacing, a trout slides across the arch of her foot—*

and you scrunch up your eyes and try to be there instead; in a lake, sinking. But one of them is unbuckling your jeans already. You throw up again, it smells like rotten apples and boil-in-the-bag curry, and when you swallow it tastes like burnt plastic. You slump further into the grass, bare thighs and ripped knicker elastic; the vomit is stuck to the side of your face and knotted in your hair.

*

It's sitting on your bed, in the dark, thinking of the prayer your granny used to teach you. Pray like this, she'd say, putting your hands together, then squashing hers over them. You'd lie on her pull-down sofa, listening, and she'd say something about heaven, something about bread every day, and there was something about no being cunts to each other, but you don't really remember the rest of it. You cover your ears, but you still hear the plates getting smashed, and your da hollering and your ma wailing, but it's muffled, like she's underwater. You spring out of bed, pacing the floor, then grab a jotter from your schoolbag and start to write. It feels like you've severed an artery, feels like you've unclogged a drain. You keep the lamp off, scared your da will see the slit of light under your door and you get dragged by the hair again. And in the prayer, there was a bit about how God was gonnae deliver us from evil, and you think, Well could you hurry the fuck up then. And the next day, you take your ma's lighter, and tear the pages of your jotter into strips, and watch your words burn in an ashtray.

*

It's bunking off school with Izzy, sitting on the sloped grass verge beside the canal, sharing a can of warm lager, watching bulldozers demolish your old tenements. Heat and dust, mounds of rubble and dirt, and you see ripped grey fragments of wallpaper as the buildings are sliced in two: walls the colour of lard, dampness as black and greasy as the arse of a chip pan. Your ma actually started to cry when she read the letter saying what was going tae happen, and you don't know why, 'cause she used to say animals in a zoo lived fucking better. Bits of grit under the lid of your eyes, the air smells like tyres are burning. You take a swig from the can and pass it to Izzy. You undo the buttons at the bottom of your shirt, tie a knot under your ribs, then wipe the sweat from your stomach with the flat of your hand. You'd be in Biology class right now – formaldehyde and frogs' legs, fallopian tubes and fertilised eggs – a large dog-eared diagram of a uterus, that to you looks like a cow skull painted pink, tacked up on the wall. Your stomach is growling. Izzy has a stale cracker in her bag, snaps it in two, and hands you a half. You chew, but it's brittle, so you both sip some lager. She makes the sign of a cross and says, In the name of the Father that's never around, Forever an Alky, Amen, and you laugh, but she doesn't.

And bricks the colour of dirty bathwater crumble and crash to the ground, and Izzy says, It's a bit sad innit? And you nod, but you're remembering the mound of used johnnies in the corner of your close every Sunday morning, dirty needles and broken necks of glass on the pavement from smashed bottles of Beck's.

A tooth lodged in a shag-pile carpet.

And you think of your da, with a tiny roach smoked to the nub, scraping muck from under his thumbnail before flicking it onto the floor; your ma out scrubbing office blocks for pennies and shabby smiles. And you think of that day you got that feeling between your legs, like a deflated balloon smeared in oil was heavy inside your pants, and you hobbled home and wiped the lump away with tissues then, without looking, flushed it down the toilet.

It is a bit sad, you say, squashing the can, before opening another from the four-pack of Tennent's. Tear it down, you think, grind every brick to powder, but you know this is a stain you'll never erase. You think of something your ma said, If these walls could talk, they wouldnae, they'd scream. Izzy makes a daisy-chain bracelet, puts it around her scarred wrist, and lies on her back. I'm bored, she yawns, we should go soon. You lie beside her, the tip of your little finger touching hers. Her eyes are closed, lank hair fanned out on the grass, she's drowsy from the jellies. A digger pounds and grinds at the concrete blocks, causing a flurry of grime and soil to swirl around you, up your nostrils and down your throat, and you splutter and cough. A torn scrap of wallpaper, of yellowed ferns that once were green, catches under your shoe. And you strain to hear Izzy's raspy breathing, it's a thin rope that you cling to, because you share the same air, you and her, you share the same stink, and you can't even remember that poem any more. Yeah, you say, leaning over to wipe the yellow drool from her mouth, we really should go.

Margaret Ries

LUCKY STRIKE

You see me in here, in my orange uniform, with my greasy hair in need of a haircut, and you judge me. I can see it in the curl of your lip, in how you're sitting in your chair. As far back as possible.

But who are you to judge me? Were you there? Do you know me? Nobody who doesn't know me and who wasn't there has a right to judge.

Hey, can I have one of those cigarettes?

Thanks.

See. Now I can judge you. What's a smart guy like you doing smoking? Smoking causes lung cancer. Didn't they teach you anything in school?

So you want to know what happened. That's why you're here, isn't it? Why you made that long, lonely drive from Tallahassee? Even after all these years, someone like you crawls out of the woodwork. Wants to try and understand how something like that could be possible. But you don't want to understand. Not really.

I've seen all the articles that have been written, repeating the same damn details until it makes you sick. *And then she slit her daughter's throat with a fishing knife. She didn't call an ambulance. She didn't call the police. Instead, she sat in her living room and watched her seven-year-old bleed to death while she smoked a Lucky Strike.*

I can't tell you how many times I've read that. The *Orlando Sentinel*, the *Tallahassee Democrat*, the *St Petersburg Times*. Even the paper of the local high school where I grew up. Every one of you acts like you're here to discover the truth about what happened that night, but in the end you all get tripped up by details and always the same damn ones. You're not even original about it.

Why is this news? Men murder their wives, rape their wives, assault, hit, burn, bite and maim their wives every second of the day, without it being news, or them serving time. Something about a mother and a child, though, now that takes people's breath away, even years later.

Even if they got the story all wrong.

I'm only talking to you for the Brownie points. The warden likes for the prison to seem open, progressive, like we're all improving, getting along with folks, ready to be reintegrated into society. To me, it's an easy way to get a pack of smokes and extra library privileges.

*

So. I was sitting out on the back porch, smoking a cigarette. Jesse was sleeping in my bed. She had been ever since I told her daddy to get lost three months and two and a half days prior. For some reason, she doted on that fool and missed having him at home, even though he hit her as often as he hit me. Maybe a little less since she was at school during the day.

I guess I'd doted on him, too. At some point.

The moon was full and lighting up the moss hanging from the trees. It was spooky, but in a pleasurable, goose-bumpy kind of way because you know nothing's really going to happen. At most, the moss will swing back and forth in the breeze like those torn curtains we had in the kitchen when I was a kid. I had flicked my cigarette into the yard and was going back inside. I went to open the screen door. Jesse was pressed against it. The sight of her gave me a fright. She'd been asleep for hours.

She was dancing back and forth on her tiptoes in her long white nightgown. I could see the bones on the tops of her feet.

'Mama! Daddy's home!'

My first thought was, it can't be true. I hadn't heard a thing, not even the squeak of the springs as Jesse got out of bed. But then I saw his big ugly shape behind her.

I yanked on the screen door so hard and so fast I pulled Jesse right along with it. How dare that son of a bitch come crawling back home? Which is exactly what I told him.

'How dare you sneak in here, scaring us both half to death? This isn't your home no more, Floyd.'

'He didn't scare me, Mama. I was happy to see him.'

'She sure was. Come right over and give me a big kiss, right here.' Floyd tapped his cheek.

He took a step forward, in the moonlight, and I realised it wasn't his fat ugly finger he was using to tap against his cheek, but his old fishing knife, the one he's always forgetting to sharpen. A shiver ran through me.

I noticed then he was wearing gloves, which was unusual, not only for the time of year, but because he's just not a glove-wearing kind of man. I felt my left leg start to twitch, like it always does when I get anxious.

'Come, on, Mama. Daddy's brought us some ice cream.'

Jesse dragged me into the living room. She wasn't lying. On the kitchen table was a big tub of Breyer's mint chocolate chip. Maybe that's why he needed the gloves, I thought. To carry the cold ice cream

I crossed my arms, trying to look fearsome. 'Nothin's changed, Floyd. You still ain't welcome here. So git.'

Jesse ran over to him and grabbed his hand. 'Oh, come on, Mama. I've been missing him so much. Can't we at least have a dish of ice cream together, like we used to?' She smiled her sweetest smile at me. 'Please, Mama?'

If only I hadn't listened to her, everything might have turned out different. But that please, together with the dimple digging deep into her cheek, always got me.

'It's just a little ice cream, Mavis. Where's the harm in that?' Floyd said, stroking Jesse's back like she was a cat he owned.

'You stay out of this, Floyd. It's none of your business. Just let me think a minute.' I glanced over at Jesse. Honest to God, if she wasn't beaming like the moon outside. Part of the reason I'd thrown the bastard out was because of how he treated her. It was like we'd never stayed up half the night, with me holding a box of frozen peas on her eye with one hand and a pack of tater tots on my own with the other. I wrapped my knuckles against my forehead. Think, think, think. It was so distracting when Floyd was around. He always got my motor running, and now he was carrying a knife to boot. I squeezed my eyes shut.

Think.

I took a deep breath. 'Okay. But only one scoop each and then it's skedaddle, Floyd. I mean it. It's gonna take more than a tub of ice cream to make amends.'

'Oh, thank you, Mama,' Jesse said.

Floyd grinned, flaunting that dimple of his own. 'It's a start, ain't it? You know how sorry I am.' Floyd scratched his stomach, working that big gut of his up and down. 'For everything.'

I got the bowls, the spoons, the scooper, and dished everybody up some ice cream.

Jesse's favourite thing in the whole world was ice cream, so she was right there beside me at the kitchen counter, her chin on her hands, saying, 'Just a little more. Oh, please, Mama.'

Floyd wasn't much interested in the ice cream. He opened the fridge.

'Want one?' he asked me.

It was tempting. Some of our best times were when we were drinking together, but it was hard enough to think now he was back. I didn't need alcohol muddling me up, too.

'No, thanks. And only one for you, too. I know what happens when you drink.'

Floyd just grinned and hooked his fingers around a couple of Buds. 'Grab my ice cream, will ya?' he said as he walked to the living room.

We had a fireplace in there. It was brick, raised up from the floor a bit like a step, where you could sit, warm your back on the fire. Floyd had made the thing himself, knocked a hole in the wall, built the chimney up through the roof, laid the brick straight and true like a professional.

He built the house too, but that was before my time. If I hadn't a seen the fireplace, I would never have believed it about the house, but I'm sure it's true. There are some things even Floyd wouldn't lie about, and construction is one of them.

It was one of those things I loved about him, when I still loved him. That that fat, rough-and-tumble man could build something as thoughtful as that fireplace. I come from way down in the state, where it's warmer. He said he didn't want me catching a chill in the winter. He even carved our initials surrounded by a heart into one of the bricks. With that dull old fishing knife. That really got me.

Jesse grabbed her bowl and plonked herself right down next to Floyd on the brick step. I perched on the couch, my bowl on my knee.

I was eyeing that bottle of beer. Floyd had opened it with his lighter and thrown back half of it before I sat down. I hadn't had a drink since I threw him out, three months and two and a half days prior.

It wasn't that I didn't want to, I did. There was nothing I loved better at the end of a long day at the dry cleaner's, the dried sweat running fresh again, than sitting out on the back porch with a cigarette and a beer. But I'd seen what it done to Floyd. Drink took a good man and turned him sour. I was trying not to go the same way. If I took even one sip, I'd be a goner.

I was nervous he was drinking, but I couldn't get my mind off that beer, sloshing back and forth like the ocean. I could almost hear it. And Floyd looked so contented every time he raised the bottle. I bet it was a really good beer.

He finished that one, and then the second one and was heading towards the fridge for a third.

'That's enough, Floyd.'

'Just one more and I'll be out of your hair. Remember that?' he said, pointing to the heart.

'Of course I do, Floyd. But scratching our initials in a brick don't mean you can come back home.'

I saw the vein in his forehead pulse big for a second, and he raised his voice. 'But this is my house.'

'I know it is, Floyd. But you're still not comin' back. Ever.'

Floyd held up his gloved hands. 'Okay, okay. Easy does it. Just thought I'd try my luck.'

He called to me from the fridge. 'Sure you don't want one?'

I'd finished my ice cream by that point and I was pretty thirsty. Ice cream always does that to me. I squeezed my eyes shut again and rapped my forehead. One two three. No. No. No.

'Sure.'

Jesse was still working her way through her mound of ice cream. She liked to collect the pieces of chocolate on the side of her bowl, eat all the ice cream, and then suck on each chip individually. A bowl of ice cream could take her all day. I'd forgotten that when I gave in to her pleas for more.

'Can't you maybe eat two chocolate chips at once? Hurry things up a bit? It's a school day tomorrow.'

Jesse smiled at me from under her bangs. 'You know I can't, Mama.'

She was right. I did know. Once she'd developed a particular ritual for something, there was no moving her. It made her feel safe. I often admired her single-mindedness, but not tonight.

I was thinking how I could get rid of Floyd and get Jesse back into bed within the next thirty minutes, when suddenly I jumped.

Floyd was behind me, holding what felt like an ice-cold beer against my neck.

'This is MY house,' he said, in that voice I knew so well, the one that's as mean and smooth as a water moccasin. The whole of me shivered, not just my neck.

I started cursing myself. Why'd I let him in, even that little toe-hold, for a couple of beers and a bowl of ice cream? Why didn't I throw him out immediately? Why didn't I call the police? Why? Why? Why?

Jesse was filling up on chocolate chips. The atmosphere was so charged I was surprised her hair didn't stand on end, but she didn't notice a thing.

I squinched my eyes shut. I didn't dare rap my forehead. Think. Think. Think.

But the only thing I could think was: This is my fault.

After what seemed like forever, Floyd flicked his knife shut. 'I'm just messin' with you, Mavis. You know that.'

It nicked my neck anyway. I guess he'd taken the time to sharpen it up, since last I saw him.

'Now I've come a mighty long way to see you. You could at least have the courtesy to have a beer with me.'

He held a beautiful brown bottle out to me. The top was off. My heart was clogging up my throat. I knew a sip of beer would be just the thing to wash it back into place.

'I said no, Floyd.'

That spot on my neck smarted, but I tried not to show it. I didn't want him to know he'd hurt me. Even by accident.

'You said "sure", Mavis. That sure sounds like yes to me.' He patted the sofa next to him. 'Come on. Sit. You're not gonna let a good beer go to waste, are ya?'

I didn't want to. I swear I didn't want to sit down on that sofa and drink that beer, but I didn't see any other way of getting him out of the house. So I did. I held the rim up to my mouth and I sucked it dry.

*

When I came to, my head was pounding and I'd slipped from the sofa to the floor. But the air was empty. I could feel it. I breathed in deep and easy.

Jesse was asleep in my lap. I didn't know how she'd gotten there. Or how I'd gotten to the floor, for that matter. I hugged her close. 'He's gone,' I whispered in her ear. 'That son of a bitch is gone.'

Something bit into my cheek.

Floyd's fishing knife. It was in my hand. And Jesse was in my arms, her throat flapping like a gill. And Floyd's words were in my brain, white and full of poison.

'Nobody kicks Floyd Carpenter out of his own house. Not without fair and righteous punishment.'

*

Nobody believed me, as I'm sure you know. Not even my own damn lawyer. I could see it in the way his eye would tick, his right one, that little bit of skin jumping whenever I started talking about Floyd. It didn't help that they couldn't find one shred of evidence that Floyd had been there that night – that son of a bitch had washed the dishes and taken the trash away with him – and lots to say he'd left the state when I threw him out, three months and two and a half days earlier. Nobody wanted to hear about the gloves or the fact that he'd lived in that house for so long his fingerprints were everywhere. I couldn't have gotten rid of every trace of him if I'd started cleaning the minute I kicked him out, and every minute since. Which I didn't, since I was a working, single mama, trying to raise my girl as best I could.

Or the fact that just because you leave a state, doesn't mean you can't come back.

All anybody could think about was me, sitting with Jesse in my lap, my fingers wrapped around that fucking knife, smoking a Lucky Strike. They didn't mention the tears or the sobs or the bruises I got when they dragged me off my little girl.

Or the fact that Lucky Strike was Floyd's brand.

Don't you see these cigarettes here? I smoke Kool.

Mark Russell

DRAMA

so we're doing the 1960s and leah who's eleven
nearly twelve says what's vietnam sir and scott
who has already turned twelve but looks about eight
says it's in korea isn't it sir and stephanie laughs
well sort of snorts and looks like she might pee herself
and i say no but it is in the far east like korea
and we look on the map i bought and tacked to the wall
and see why north vietnam was supported by china
but not quite why south vietnam was supported by the usa
and then rab whose name is robbie but he prefers rab
spots korea and says look there's a north and a south
just like that vietnam hingy and thomas says
wasn't there a war there too and aiden says shut up
twatface and I have to send him out to mrs lennon
and thomas says it again and we see that north korea
was supported by china and that the americans found
another way of fighting another war a long way from home
and then katie who is very quiet most of the time
says no that wasn't in the past because it's happening
today it's happening now she saw it on her phone
and that we're all going to die tomorrow or the day after
and both rebeccas stand up waving their hands shouting
we're not are we sir we're not are we we're not going to die
tomorrow are we sir and I say no but what would we do if
we thought we were going to die tomorrow how would we feel
maybe we can make a play about it let's get into groups

J. David Simons

REMEMBER FROM WHERE YOU CAME

Tomasz scraped the razor across one cheek then down under his chin, following the droop of a sagging jowl fattened on a diet of venison, boar and jugged hare. He flicked the foam into the sink, glimpsed his sleeping wife in the mirror, her nightgown tangled up around her haunches, her breathing heavy like the throaty nicker of an ageing mare. He licked his lips. Only a half-day's work until he could take his gun and dog out into the forest.

He dressed quickly, fried up a breakfast of bacon on a slab of black bread washed down with a mug of beer. He prepared a flask of coffee, wrapped himself up in his heaviest jacket, fed the dog the last of the pig rinds, gave his wife a light slap across her buttocks.

Magda groaned, moved on the bed so her gown rose even higher on her thighs. 'Go to hell,' she mumbled as she shifted further away from him.

It was still dark when he stepped outside, frost on the ground, the chill nipping his cheeks, scraping at his nostrils. He didn't have to wait long. The church clock lurched to half past six and right on time the shiny, lit-up work-bus swept round the corner, hissed to a stop level with his feet, the front door already opening to let him in. He gave a half-salute to Jerzy the driver, then swung himself up the aisle, hands gripping the back of each seat until he reached his usual spot, settled down. As usual, he was the only passenger. He poured himself a cup of coffee, unfolded the previous day's newspaper. This was his favourite time, these precious twenty minutes before the bus arrived at the next town.

For here they came, those gaggling girls with their gossip and their make-up still to be plastered on. Quite an art, Tomasz thought, given the sway of the bus, with a glance to their skinny legs. The girls ignored him, puckered their lips in a readiness to be reddened, ready to be kissed by a man much younger than he. Yet, he could still feel the longing, why shouldn't he? The last time he had felt Magda's mouth on his own, Lech Wałęsa was still president of this ruin of a country. Most of these girls worked in the kitchen, reception or in the gift shop, the tour guides among them keeping their smart uniforms to themselves further up the bus. He snapped at his newspaper, scrunched down further into his jacket.

The sun was up and the dew was glinting off the rime on the flat fields by the time the sentry boxes came into view. So many of them, each one marking another fifty yards closer to the end of his daily journey, the looming barracks still holding the power to silence all the passengers on board. Jerzy turned down the radio as the bus swung into the main avenue. Tomasz glanced at the famous sign over the gateway welcoming him as it did every morning. 'Arbeit Macht Frei.'

Tomasz was born after the war, during the coldest winter of the century. His father said if his baby son could survive this freeze, he could survive anything. His father rarely spoke about the war, rarely spoke at all. Tomasz could hardly blame him, his parents had spent years breathing in the ashes of thousands of cremated souls, humming out the sound of tortured screams. The old man had been a woodsman, supplying firewood for the village, then to the Nazis, then to the Russians, then to the villagers again. 'I don't care who I sell to,' his father said. 'As long as I can feed my family.' Tomasz would have been a woodsman too if he hadn't hurt his back, flattened by a tree his father had felled. He ended up upgrading his driving skills so he could steer the school bus around the villages. It was Jerzy who had got him this job, the pay was much better, he liked the fact he was working for World Cultural Heritage.

It was easy, mindless work, driving his own busload of tourists the two kilometres from A to B. Or at least that's what the staff called two of the most horrific destinations on earth. From Auschwitz to Buchenwald. Then back again. Four trips an hour, twenty-four trips a day, fifty minutes at the end to sweep the inside of the bus, hose it down, fill it up with diesel, lunch in the canteen in between. A to B was a straight road too, following the line of the disused railway track, hardly a chance to move into top gear before he had to slow down again. Never any trouble, the tourists nice and respectful by the time they reached him, softened up and quietened down by a walk through torture chambers, punishment cells, warehouses stacked with shoes and prayer shawls. When he had first started work here, he used to pay his passengers a bit of attention, giving each of them a little nod of compassion as they stepped on board. Now he didn't even bother, just sat there with the engine ticking over nicely, his cup of coffee resting on his belly. He might hear a few of them sobbing at the back, but a little pressure on the accelerator soon drowned them out. He would just scratch his cheek, look off beyond the barracks, the electric fences and the sentry boxes to the faraway forests where he imagined the boar wallowing in their muddy pools.

On this morning, his shift started with three trips from A to B and back again with the usual mix of nationalities. These were the independent travellers, the ones who wanted to wander around by themselves, too self-absorbed or too mean to pay for a guide. The group tours didn't start until around ten-thirty, he had seen the roster already, annoyed with his assignment on this day when he wanted things to go just right. He went to complain to Madame Czarnecka in administration.

'You know I don't do the Israelis,' he told her. 'Especially the schoolkids.'

Madame Czarnecka counted off her problems on bony fingers. 'Andrzej is sick. So is Konrad. Lodzia has to look after her children. Kazik hasn't turned up. Today you do the Israelis.'

He looked down the list again. 'Give me this lot. The synagogue group from New York.'

'Too late. They've gone out with Dodek.'

He stared at her but she locked her arms as a fortress against him. 'I don't understand you, Tomasz. Jews. Israelis. What's the difference?'

There were about thirty of them, probably in their last year of high school before the army took them. Other groups were usually sombre and subdued, dressed-down for the visit, shocked into silence by the time they reached Tomasz. But the Israelis were different, especially the younger ones. They were often noisy and colourfully dressed, some of them even draped themselves in the blue-and-white of their national flag. That was what he hated about them. As if somehow this was their tragedy and no one else's. The other drivers told him not to get too upset. After all, the Holocaust was something that had been hammered into these poor kids since birth. This visit was as natural to them as a trip to Disneyland for those brought up on Mickey Mouse, rather than tales of the Gestapo knocking at their door.

This morning's group was particularly raucous, a lot of boy–girl baiting as they clambered on board, one youngster knocking against Tomasz's shoulder, not even bothering to apologise. Tomasz grunted, turned down the heating, let them cool off in more ways than one. Beata the tour guide picked up the microphone, tried to quieten them but most of them were not listening, having abandoned the tour's audio headsets for their own personal music. Tomasz opened up the rear exit to let in the chilled air, revved up the engine, glanced at the noisy horde in his mirror, saw a couple of teachers sitting together midway down the aisle, chatting away, ignoring the ruckus going on all around them. Beata tried again with her microphone but quickly gave up, turned round to Tomasz with an exasperated look.

'I'm not moving until they sit,' he said, then went back to reading his newspaper.

Beata brought the microphone close to her lips. 'Will you please sit down,' she called out in Hebrew. 'Please sit.'

The riotous behaviour continued. Tomasz almost felt obliged to grab the microphone himself, deliver his own personal message for them to shut up. He didn't want to be late. He had a bus to catch himself. There was wild boar to kill.

He looked up from his paper, caught his first glimpse of her in his interior mirror, striding up the aisle in her grey fur hat, dark fitted coat nipped up tight at the collar, with all the haughty grace of one of those elegant women he'd seen strolling along Warsaw's Nowy Świat. He hadn't noticed her before, she must have slipped in through the rear door when he had opened it to let in the cold. This Israeli teacher was nothing like the fair-haired women of his own nation with their cold eyes and even colder hearts. And nothing like the pale Jewesses he associated with the Diaspora. This woman was a dark-skinned, brown-eyed Mediterranean beauty. She snatched the microphone from Beata, reeled off some phrases in Hebrew.

Tomasz glanced again at his mirror. Everyone had stopped talking. Those who had been standing were sinking slowly back into their seats. The two teachers raised themselves up slightly, looked towards their lone colleague with the microphone. She stood just off to his side, her hip almost touching his shoulder. He could hear her breathing, he could smell her scent. She returned the microphone to Beata. And as she did so, she lost her balance slightly on the top step, gripped Tomasz's upper arm to stop herself from falling. He felt the pressure of her grasp through his jacket and then as a judder right down his body. She smiled at him.

'I'm sorry,' she said in English.

He felt himself redden, almost knocking over his coffee cup with a heave of his belly. When had he last blushed to the smile of a beautiful woman? Probably when Lech Wałęsa was still president of this dungheap of a country. He observed her again in his mirror as she walked back down the silent aisle to her seat, waited until she had settled. He then shivered himself into alertness, moved the bus through the gears.

'What did she say to them?' he asked Beata.

'To keep quiet.'

'It was more than that.'

'She said – *remember from where you came*. That was all. Remember from where you came.'

*

Tomasz stretched his back, aching from so many hours at the wheel, gazed up to the sky through the ceiling of branches. A perfect afternoon for hunting. A little bit of rain earlier on to fill up the wallowing pools and now not a whiff of wind to alert the boars' sensitive snouts. The forest always reminded him of his father. As soon as he stepped foot in it, the smell of the loam was enough to set him off, bringing back the sight of the old man with his shouldered axe, always moving slightly ahead until his withered lungs

began to slow him down. It was the cigarettes that killed his father
in the end although his mother said it was from breathing in the
wind-blown ash from the furnaces he had fuelled. A punishment
from God.

He called for his hound, Bazyli, then began his usual routine,
checking the tree barks for evidence of rubbing, the soil for signs
of rooting. Bazyli was also adept at picking up spots where the boar
had been, sniffing the soil like a demented vacuum cleaner, anxious
to please his master with a detected scent. Back in the summer, he
had built two new huts, each placed in a different part of the forest
beside potential wallowing pools. The problem was deciding which
one to shoot from today. He had hoped it wasn't going to be the one
furthest away but the various telltale signs on the trees and in the
soil had pointed him in that general direction until after struggling
high into the forest, he eventually settled himself down there, panting
and hungry. He looked at his watch. Almost four o'clock. He reckoned
on another two hours and the boar would be out just before dusk.

The platform for the hut was built on stilts with a few rickety steps
for access, more as a hiding place rather than for protection against
a full-on charge. Three walls, front and to the sides, each with their
own large viewing window, a camouflage of branches and a ledge
just at the right height to take the lean of a rifle barrel. There were
a few dirty cushions scattered around, a pile of withered hunting
magazines, a dwindled stack of sardine tins, a few empty plastic
bottles sliced open to catch the rain. Tomasz heaved himself into a
sitting position with a good view of the wallow about thirty feet
away, took out the foil wrap of beef sandwiches Magda had made
up for him.

Friends who weren't hunters used to say to him it must be good
to be out there in the woods by yourself, all that time to think. But
the truth was he never really thought about anything. At least, not
anything significant. He might ponder the previous evening's football
results but that was about it. He just sat there with his eyes, ears and
Winchester primed for the kill, thinking of nothing. It had been the
same with his father. When as a boy he had sat with him, watching
the old man's expressionless blue-grey eyes staring out at the woods,

he remembered asking him for his thoughts. 'Doesn't help a man to dwell too much on anything,' his father had replied. Tomasz only ever once probed further to ask about what had happened during the war. The old man had shuddered then, spat out some loose tobacco from his roll-up. 'Well, they got what they wanted,' he had said bitterly. 'Who got what?' Tomasz asked. 'You know. They got their country. Out there in Palestine.'

But as he sat there looking out into the forest, his Winchester resting on the ledge, it wasn't memories of his father that came to him. It was the image of the Israeli teacher that kept nudging for his attention. He even touched his arm where she had placed her own hand that very morning. She had caused such an ache inside of him that at one point, he thought he should just unbutton himself there and then, relieve himself like he used to do when he was a teenager. But then he saw Bazyli's ears prick up, and he hunkered down into a silence. He knew he had to keep still, hold his breathing shallow, quieten the heart and hope the breeze didn't carry the scent of man or dog. Wild boar might be short-sighted but their sense of hearing and smell was acute. Bazyli stirred again and Tomasz felt his heart lurch on hearing the crumple of leaves and broken branches as the giant hulk of meat and tusk came rushing through the trees.

It was a prize target, a mature hog, must have weighed in at more than a hundred kilos. The beast went straight for the mud pool, almost childlike in its joy as it sank into the wallow. Tomasz followed the animal with the sight of his rifle, his arms shaking with excitement as he eased his finger over the trigger. Such ugly creatures, all out of proportion, with their heavy bodies on those skinny legs, the flared tusks, the bristled hide and those horrible snouts. The more of these grotesque animals he could slaughter the better.

He ran his tongue over his dry lips. He would wait until the boar was fully broadside before he fired, aiming forward and low where the vital organs were lodged. That way if he caught it too high then at least he would shatter a shoulder, kill the collapsed body quick with a follow-up shot. What he didn't want was the beast to turn head-on. Then he would have to go for the brain where the skull was thick and no easy target.

He adjusted his stance ever so slightly, moving his leg where he had a slight cramp. His foot hit a couple of empty tins. He had hardly made a sound but that hog picked up the noise straight away, turned quickly towards its source. 'Damn,' Tomasz hissed.

The beast moved out of the mud pool, its tiny eyes staring right at him, snout down with those sharp tusks flaring. He lodged the rifle butt harder into his shoulder as he tried to fix the animal's head in his sight with his trembling hands. What was happening to him? He was an experienced hunter with hundreds of kills under his belt yet his composure was all over the place. He took his forward grip off the rifle, placed it over his racing heart. Was he about to have some kind of seizure? The boar started to drive towards the hut. Tiny legs carrying such a heavy weight yet the animal could move swift across the ground. He gripped the rifle again. He had to hit the animal cleanly right through its skull. He focused on the bobbing target through his sights and as the beast charged towards him, bringing with it the possibility of imminent death, he remembered from where he came.

Mark Ryan Smith

WHALER'S TESTAMENT

Carefully oiled and swaddled in hessian,
three rafters take the weight.

The barn smells of earth and tarred sarking;
wooden uprights smoothed by animal flanks

when they stowed them here in winter,
the dung packed thick by spring.

He hated shovelling but did it anyway,
working the croft was never his thing –

then neither was the sea, if truth be told,
but he found it easier being away

from the strings around wrists
of genealogies and inherited land.

And now he'll pass it on in turn,
a parcel of deeds and responsibilities

that eighty-nine years has dwindled into.
But he'll keep the harpoon.

He takes the twine from the neck of the sack
and rubs away the oil. The steel still bright

underneath, the edge still sharp for the big fish
he might see yet.

C. A. Steed

THE LAST DOOR

'One day, you will be old enough to start reading fairy tales again.'
—C. S. Lewis, *The Lion, The Witch and the Wardrobe*

My grandmother lives in a house without doors. I used to think that was normal, when I was little – that all grandmothers lived in windy, draughty houses with the doors missing from all the rooms and wardrobes.

Inside her house, there are long hallways and empty rooms, around which the wind whistles and blows and whispers. The doorways are gaps, like the places left behind when teeth fall out. There are still hinges in the frames, and as a child I used to play with them, opening and shutting them as though they were tiny, shiny little doors themselves. I liked the firm little click they made when you pushed them shut with a finger. The cupboards and wardrobes are also doorless, so you can see in to the clothes kept swinging on hangers inside. There is never much in the wardrobes, so you can easily see their wooden backs. They did not make for particularly good hiding places.

Granny Susie is not a normal grandmother in a lot of ways. She doesn't bake, or put up on her fridge your laboriously made finger paintings. She isn't physically affectionate, though she is gentle in her own way. She is tall and thin, with long grey hair she wears wound into a bun. My mum told me once that her hair is so long it falls to her feet.

We didn't visit often when I was a child, because my father didn't like Granny Susie. He called her a 'mad old bat' and was grumpy and silent when we did make one of our infrequent trips to her house. He'd wear two jumpers and a scarf indoors, and make pointed comments about how cold and draughty the house was. Mum's lips would get tighter and tighter, and they'd have a raging argument in the car on the way home. I hated this part of our visits.

But I loved seeing Granny Susie. There's something about adults who are utterly indifferent to other adults that is enormously appealing to a child. She spent much more time talking to me than she did my parents, and she spoke to me just as you would an equal. She made me feel I was the most important person in the world. In that way, she was the perfect grandmother.

There is only one door in her house, the front door, and even that is permanently wedged open with a brick. During our visits, my mother and Granny Susie would have regular arguments over the door being open all the time, Mum pointing out that murderers and thieves and WHO KNEW WHAT ELSE could walk right in whenever they pleased. Granny Susie, in her turn, would point out that she'd lived like that for years and had never had a problem. Her house, in fact, was so remote that murderers and thieves were in generally short supply, and she was far safer than we were in the city, where such people abounded. At this point in the argument my mother would throw up her hands and give up, Granny Susie would sniff and drink her black tea, and my dad would put on another scarf.

Granny Susie lives mostly in the kitchen, which is the only room in the house that is anything like warm. She has a big old Aga that hums with heat, and my favourite seat in the house is the straight-backed chair that sits in a little alcove beside the stove. My dad usually took that seat, though.

The kitchen is scrupulously clean, and, like the rest of the house, there are no paintings or photographs on the walls. There are two shelves of books, old, boring-looking tomes with dusty titles like *Hermeneutics of Religious Devotion*, and *On Belief in the Later Middle Ages*. They don't have any pictures.

The kitchen window looks out on the foothill of the mountain known as 'the Caer' – 'the fortress' in Welsh. It is tall and forbidding, and doesn't invite an afternoon's scramble up to the peak, like the mountain (really just a hill) that I live near in Edinburgh does.

It took hours and hours for us to drive to Granny Susie's. These drives were long and boring, because although I always took a stock of suitable paperbacks for such a journey (the Famous Five and the Secret Seven, mostly – I was a sucker for adventure), we usually made the trip overnight. I would try to read in the snatches of light provided by streetlights, and even this unsatisfying gobbling sentence by sentence was preferable to the achingly long distances through the country, where there were no streetlights. The headlights of passing cars went by too fast to even read a word at a time (though I did try). Eventually, I would fall into an uncomfortable, lolling-headed sleep, to be woken by the crunch of gravel as we finally pulled into Granny Susie's drive.

Once, we took the train. Dad had hurt his back trying to move some furniture and said he couldn't drive the whole way. The train was amazing – I could walk up and down the aisles, ladies came past regularly with carts filled with cans of fizzy juice and biscuits that sufficient whining procured, and there were lights so I could read as much as I wanted – but I was sworn to absolute secrecy by Mum and Dad. A rare united front, they told me in no uncertain terms that I was never to tell Granny Susie that we'd come by train. Why, I'd asked. Never mind why, I was told. It'll upset her. So just don't.

I didn't tell her, but it was still my fault she found out. I'd been curled up on the second-best chair in the house (a winged armchair in the living room, facing the window with its back to the empty doorway) deep in my latest Enid Blyton. So I didn't hear Granny Susie come in the room, and I didn't hear her footsteps stop abruptly when she saw what was in my hands, and I only barely heard her when she spoke. Without looking up from my page, I said, 'What, Granny Susie?' in kind of an irritable way. I didn't like being disturbed when I was reading.

'What,' she said, 'is that?' I glanced over at her. She was looking at my hands.

'It's my book,' I said.

'No,' she said. 'Not your book. *That.*' And she pointed to the fingers of my right hand, between which was resting the bright orange train ticket I'd been using as a bookmark.

That was a horrible visit. Granny Susie, usually so calm and controlled, shouting at my mother in the next room, saying, 'But you *promised.* You promised to *never,*' over and over again, and my mother trying desperately to reason with her. My dad tried to help at first, talking in a smooth, aggressively reasonable sort of voice, the kind you use with people who are threatening to fling themselves off the roof of a building, but when that didn't work he gave up and went and lay on the back seat of Granny Susie's ancient car with the heater running full blast. I went and sat in one of the doorless wardrobes, my head buffeted by swinging coats, my fingers pressed in my ears and my book lying abandoned by the chair in the front room.

Later, much later, my mum came to find me. The sun had travelled across the walls and floor, and extinguished itself past the window so that the room was dark. I heard my mum's footsteps (she walked more softly than Granny Susie or Dad), then her knees clicking as she squatted down. 'Oof,' she said. 'Better not let Granny catch you in here. Come on.'

I wiped at long-dry eyes as I stood. 'I'm sorry,' I said miserably.

'Oh, it's not your fault,' said Mum. She put an arm around my shoulders. 'It's not anyone's fault, really.' She told me, then, how Granny Susie's entire family – parents, two brothers, one sister and a cousin – had died in a train crash when she was only twenty-one.

'What, all of them? All at once?'

'All of them. All at once,' my mother confirmed. I thought about how sad Granny Susie must have been, how awful it must be to be alone in the world like that.

'And that's the reason she doesn't like us going on trains?'

Mum sighed. 'It's the reason for a lot of things, Cee-Cee.' I'd known that I was named for my grandmother's sister, but I hadn't known what had happened to her. 'Granny was a bit of a socialite when she was young, but the accident . . . well, it changed her.'

We had to take the train home, of course. The first thing Mum did when we arrived was to find a payphone and call my grandmother. 'Mum?' she said into the receiver, her knuckles white around its black plastic. 'That's us home. We're all safe.'

She listened, then hung the phone back on its hook. She saw my look, and shrugged. Dad was gesturing red-faced from the taxi rank.

When I was older, around sixteen, I started going to visit Granny Susie by myself. I couldn't drive, and of course I couldn't take the

train, so I got a couple of long-haul buses to get from Edinburgh to
Swansea, then a local bus to the stop nearest her house, then walked
the last mile or so. I liked these journeys – I took crisps, juice, a
supply of paperbacks and a little torch to read them with when it
got dark – and I felt like an adventurer, setting off out into the world
with only what I carried on my back.

Granny Susie was, I think, always glad to see me. I'd arrive on
the second day of school holidays, generally damp and crumpled
from my long journey, and she'd have made up a bed for me in
one of the less chillier rooms, and there would be tea and scones
ready and waiting for me in the kitchen. She'd pile the scones with
jam and cream – the only indulgence I really remember her having
and we'd talk and talk in the warmth of the kitchen.

I went through a religious phase, when I was about nineteen, and
I remember it being the only thing I'd ever told her that she openly
disapproved of. Granny Susie had looked down into her black tea,
and said, 'Don't trust gods, Lucy. They want all of your heart and
none of your mind, and you have a fine mind.' It was the only time
I can remember that she used my proper name.

She'd told me I had a fine mind before. I had been little, maybe
six or seven, and I was reading Roald Dahl's *The Witches* for the
umpteenth time. She'd asked me what I was reading, and I'd launched
into a detailed summation of the plot. About halfway through,
when I'd got to the bit where the boys are turned into mice by
the terrifying, gruesome crowd of bald, crowing witches, she
stopped me.

'You know that it's not real, don't you, Cee-Cee?' Cee-Cee was
the nickname she had given me, and which the rest of my family
ultimately adopted.

'Of course, Granny,' I said. 'It's just in the book.'

'That's right,' she said. She had a strange, faraway look in her eyes.
'It's important to know the difference between reality and funny
games.'

'I know when it's just playing,' I said, uncomfortable. She looked
at me, and the distance in her eyes receded. She smiled at me, gentle.

'Of course you do,' she said. 'You have a fine mind.'

It was Granny Susie who encouraged me to go to university to study philosophy, which Dad had hooted at and Mum had worried about. So, you're going to spend four years *thinking*, Dad had snorted. What kind of job could you get with a degree in philosophy, Mum had worried. But Granny Susie had told me not to worry about jobs, and that to spend four years thinking was a fine use for a mind like mine.

As I became wrapped up in life at university, I visited less and less. I did still get down to her once or twice a year, sometimes driving, now I had my licence and the occasional use of Mum's car, sometimes going by plane if there was a cheap flight, sometimes, even, going by rail. I was always careful to rip up and throw away my ticket as soon as I got off the train, though.

One New Year, when I'd broken up with the latest boyfriend and didn't, therefore, feel like going to the party where he and all our mutual friends would be, I decamped to Granny Susie's house in Wales, at the foot of the Caer mountain. I felt like being in a fortress, even if it was a draughty and empty fortress for the most part. I remember running my finger over the spines of the books in her kitchen while she busied herself at the stove. My finger stopped on one I hadn't noticed before, one which didn't seem to belong to the other dry volumes. It was called *Possible Impossibilities*, by a Professor Digory Kirke, and on the lower end of the spine was an embossed silver apple. 'What's this one?' I asked.

She turned, wiping her hands on a tea-towel. Slowly, she reached out and took the book from me. Her fingers trailed down the cover, stroked the closed page edges, paused on the letters of the author's name.

'I lived with him, for a while,' she said, almost inaudibly.

'Professor Kirke?' I asked. 'When did you live with him?'

'When I was just a girl. About – oh, twelve?' She sat at the table, still gripping the book. I sat too, hardly daring to breathe. She never spoke about her life, never told me anything of herself as a child. I felt like a hunter, spying a fawn in the far reaches of the forest. If

I was silent and still, perhaps it would come close enough that I could bring it down with my bow and arrow. But if I moved or spoke at the wrong time, it would startle and flee.

'My brothers and sister and I were sent to live with him, because of the war. He lived in a great old house in the country, and he had this awful grumpy housekeeper we used to hide from.'

'Where did you hide?' I asked.

'In the wardrobe,' she said distantly. She stood up and replaced the book on the shelf, and I sensed the subject was closed.

She's ill, now. A neighbour, concerned that he hadn't seen her make her usual walk to the nearest village's little general store for a couple of mornings, went to her house and let himself in the – of course – open front door. She was in the kitchen, lying next to the Aga, which probably saved her. If she'd fallen in another part of the house, the cold might have been enough to finish her off over the two nights and two days she had lain there, cursing the stool which had shifted – she said – under her foot as she stepped on it to reach a high shelf.

I went to see her in hospital, with Mum. It was hard because she was confused and didn't seem to know quite who Mum and I were. She thought Mum's name was Jill, and although she called me Lucy we realised after a while that she thought I was her long-dead little sister. She asked where our brothers were ('Where's Peter, Lucy? Where's Ed?'), and I told her that I was an only child. She shook her head and said, 'What a wonderful memory you have! Fancy you still playing those funny games you used to play when we were children.' She smiled when she said it, but looked angry, almost.

I had begun my PhD, but I applied to the university for compassionate leave and have spent the last two weeks here, visiting all the hours the hospital will allow and staying along the road in an Airbnb in the hours that they won't. Granny is in a room on her own, and I've made the nurses promise to keep the door open. They can see it makes her calmer, so they do.

Her hand is paper-thin, and when I hold it I feel like I'm holding air. She is so frail, now. She asks me over and over if the door to the wardrobe is closed, and I assure her that it isn't. There is no wardrobe in her room. The hospital chaplain, a kind-eyed imam, came in this morning to ask if she needed any spiritual comfort. Granny Susie, enjoying a brief lucid period, fixed him with a sharp eye and told him she had no need of comfort from any god. Then she got confused again, because she told me once he had left not to let any more 'Calormen' in. It sounds like an old racist term, which isn't like her.

It's dark outside, and the nurses will soon be in to shoo me away. Granny Susie is dozing, and I am reading my book. It's Plato's *The Republic* – I'm supposed to be teaching it later this semester. There is movement, and I look up to see Granny Susie trying to sit up. I help her, and hold a glass of water to her lips. She nods at my book, sinking back onto her pillows. She says something about caves.

'The Allegory of the Cave, Granny?'

'Mm.' She seems with it. 'You believe it?'

I settle back in my chair. This is like the conversations we used to have around her kitchen table, and I wish I could pull this familiar moment around myself like a blanket. 'I think it perfectly describes the process of growing up,' I say. She raises an eyebrow, so I continue. 'When we're young, the world around us is limited to our immediate experience and understanding. As we age, our world expands and we see that things we previously believed to be the truth, to be reality, are not as we had perceived.'

Granny Susie nods. 'That's what I've always been afraid of,' she whispers.

'Afraid of?'

Her fingers grasp at the bedcovers. 'Suppose that a reality you had grown out of was, in fact, real,' she says. 'Suppose that all this,' she gestures with a weak hand, 'is a shadow within a shadow? Suppose we live in the Shadowlands?'

'This is real, Granny,' I say, taking her hand. She is pale, shaking.

'I wish that were true,' she whispers. I have to bend my head to hear her. 'I wish that were true, but I know that when I die I'll be taken to his country.'

'Whose country, Granny?'

She turns away from me and says something that sounds like *he's lying*, or maybe it's *the lion*. But neither makes any sense.

'I've tried so hard to stay away from him,' she continues in a whisper, 'though I desperately – desperately – want to see them all again. But I can't go, you see. I'm not suited. Nylons, lipstick and invitations. So who knows where he'll send me?'

I have no idea how to comfort her. 'You're not going anywhere,' I say.

The light from the lamp at her bedside catches and illuminates the tears filling her lower lids. Her eyes gleam with them. 'I was on that train,' she says. 'I was supposed to be on it. Lucy said it was my last chance to go with them. He'd come in a dream and told her what they had to do. But I got off at the station before, when they weren't looking. I couldn't take the risk. Who wants to go to a God that doesn't want them? He was so terrible when he was angry . . .'

Her voice fails, and she closes her eyes. In a moment she is asleep. I watch her, troubled. I don't know why she thinks God is angry with her – because she cheated death on that train? – but how terrifying it must be to face your mortality when you believe that a great and terrible God is waiting for you on the other side.

Later, I am back in my little Airbnb, holding the silent mobile I have just finished using to tell my mum that Granny has passed away. The last few hours are a blur of hospital corridors, kind but busy nurses, and incomprehensible forms. The last door, finally, has closed behind Granny Susie, and I will never be able to ask her why she thought God was angry with her. I will never know what she thought she had done.

I do know what I hope, if not what I believe. I hope that, if there is some kind of life after death, it is like a gripping adventure story that you live in forever. That goes on endlessly, with only fun and excitement, and no cruel and angry gods, and in which every chapter is better than the one before.

Margaret Stewart

ORION'S MOUTH

I want all the stars, not just Orion leaning sideways on the cold Asda car park making pale reflections on shopping trolleys. I want the prickling of faint light-years on my skin instead of harling. I want the geometry of the great floating spaces between planets, not warm cider and the thick of boys' tongues.

When I grow up I want to be an astronaut. When I grew up I still wanted to be an astronaut. I will never be the pilot, my pupils are the wrong shape, my focal length too long to project non-blurry images into my brain. What if I was flying a fighter jet and my glasses fell off? What if my contact lenses fell out? That's what the RAF recruiter tells me later. No, I will be the Mission Specialist; tethered to the shuttle and armed with a reciprocating spanner to adjust the telescope, to point the antennas back to Earth and beam our experiments to mission control. The wrong type of spanner won't absorb momentum, will continue to obey equal and opposite forces and send me spinning away into the black. My helmet is toughened glass, my suit articulated like the bendy bit of a straw. I am free to pull myself over the carapace of the station, past the delicate gold foil protecting the electronics, crinkling and thin like sweet wrappers without sound.

My first telescope is red plastic Fisher-Price and I watch the moon wobble through suburban double glazing, craters swinging in and out of view between flat roofs and pilot lights. My second telescope is from the Argos catalogue, requires oil to be dripped very carefully into its threads, to be done outside because if my mum has told me once she's told me a thousand times to be careful of the carpet. With the Argos telescope you can see Saturn, you can see its rings bright against the black, you can see at least two moons echoing the fainter stars behind. With the Argos telescope you need to wear fingerless gloves and put a bit of red plastic from a Quality Street wrapper over your torch so that you can read the star chart without ruining your night vision. Mum will put my gloves on the radiator to warm

them up and bring me hot chocolate made in a pan and not in the
microwave, just the way I like it.

*

It is the second week of secondary school. Fourth-year boys push
the window out the back of the bus, a double-decker, someone could
have been killed. They light streams of deodorant on fire, my shoe-
laces singed, carefully chosen pencil case blackened. Gas on fire, like
plasma, a different state of matter, so hot that the atoms won't stay
together. The scabbard on Orion's belt is a nebula, a glimmer made
of dust and plasma at a million degrees Celsius, twelve million light-
years across. The police come and make us stay on the bus. My mum
and Anna's mum get worried and come looking for us in the car.

'What do you think two eleven-year-old girls have got to do with
it?' Mum is shouting. The police let us get off the bus. We didn't see
anything, I don't know where the stain on my blazer is from, I don't
know about the crocodile clips yet. We drive to the shops and get
yum-yums but Anna has to go for piano practice so she can't come
round after. I pick the burned bits off my pencil case, snip the charred
ends off my shoelaces. I have matches but don't need deodorant yet
so I can't make my own plasma.

*

A crust of ice shifts and grinds in the Saturn light, methane boils up
and smokes past my helmet. There are nine icy moons in the Solar
System, and nine planets. Comets are made of ice too, dirty with
dust and soot and carbon and frozen as solid as cold iron until they
get close enough to the sun and start to boil. A good packed snowball
with a chuckie inside it can be hard enough to break the skin, make
your nose bleed, break your glasses. Mum goes up to the school even
though I don't want her to, Ryan Cooper is made to apologise and
pay for the glasses. Ryan's dad asks him what he has to say for himself.

'It was an accident,' Ryan says, 'I didn't mean to hit her. Not in the
face.' His eyes glitter. We are in the rector's office and I've never been
there before, I've never seen Ryan not wearing school uniform. The
rector bans snowball fights and it is my fault.

In Geography Miss McCluskie has gone to find the TV trolley and all the boys are going around comparing the size of their hands and sniggering. I am drawing the catchment area of the River Nile when Gemma Gibbs pulls me up out of my chair and presses her palm to mine like we're doing a high five and got glued together. She's the only girl in the year taller than me. My fingers stretch above her nails, which are flaked with black polish, mine are bitten and bare.

'Jesus,' she says. 'Massive. Your hole must be the size of a bucket.' I freeze, hot and thick and blushing, just standing there with the plastic of the chair digging into the back of my tights and I don't really know what she's talking about, but I know it's bad. I'm trying to think of something cool to say like, Oh Ha Ha but the whole class erupts laughing and before I can do anything there is so much noise Mrs Taylor comes in from the class next door and sends Gemma out for being in hysterics. I get one hundred per cent for my drawing of the Nile.

*

I win the second-year prize for RE because I am the only pupil in the whole year who handed in their homework, even the other good kids like Anna. In third-year prizegiving I get Maths, English, Physics, Chemistry and Geography and Anna gets Art.

Red dust squeaks like snow under my boots, footprints ridged and sharp with shadows the way they only look in places without an atmosphere. I bounce when I walk, gravity isn't as good on Mars, it's harder to be heavy. Dad says it's puppy fat, makes jokes about jelly bums wibbly wobbly. I put glow-in-the-dark plastic stars all over my ceiling but I can't see them without my glasses on. I have a poster of Mulder on my bedroom wall but I dream about Scully.

Space is supposed to smell like lighter fluid and electrical burning, a hot kind of metal smell. I am trying not to smell of roll-ups and vanilla tobacco before I get home. There is frost crusting the Asda car park, grit salting the carefully drawn biro spirals on my trainers. They're the wrong trainers anyway, the wrong jacket, the wrong jeans. Anne-Marie Stuart said I have no ankles, the bone doesn't even stick out, weird. I start wearing trousers to school and jeans to the car park on Fridays. Adam is here and his brother bought him the cider. We smoke and he points out Orion and I don't say anything until we're kissing and he makes some serious efforts to get my bra off and then he walks me home. My dad doesn't like Adam because he has long hair and an earring. 'Like a girl,' Dad says, and I go up to my room before he can smell the tobacco.

*

Fourth year I get Maths, English, Geography and Physics but Alison gets Chemistry. Gemma Gibbs gets pregnant. I watch the freshwater geysers on Enceladus spatter the windshield of my buggy as I bounce from crater to crater, carefully plotting the path to the base. I stay in on Friday nights to study and I take out my old red telescope and watch the stars through the window and I want them even more. I learn how to do the maths that will fling me out past Jupiter's gravity well, the same maths that works when a ball bounces or a car turns a corner. I learn how light is a wave and a particle at the same time, how it bends towards mass, how you can write that out in exams and it might bend your own path, away from here.

*

Now there are eight planets in the Solar System and I am not an astronaut. Pluto has been demoted to an icy body and I fail second-year university maths, twice. I switch to geology and look down instead of up, catch myself in leaps of time rather than space, in the grit of coal-flecked sandstone that proves a million years of a twisting river drying and flooding and drying again.

Simon Sylvester

THE FEW POOR HOUSES OF MY SANNDABHAIG

I woke to find a sky of steel and shredded fish and thought – yes – I am here again, in my own time, whatever time that is, and the sky is the same sky I have always known, and it could never be anything else. Like a moth from a cocoon, I let the air wash across me, wake me, call me from slumber and bring me to life. Sounds, no sounds. Bees. Surf. Lapwings on the shore. A click. A click. A click. My fingers had rusted into crooks. My knees were full of powder. It felt like hours before I could move, and hours more without it hurting, all snaps and sharps between my ribs. When I did move, and could twist a hand to examine the fingers, I found them adorned with rings of copper and silver. Bangles, too, clicking about the balls of my wrists. Thin arms. A growling in my belly and again, a click, a click, a click. After so long asleep, I stretched out long, enjoying the prickles of feeling.

'Hey. You're awake?'

A man's voice, warm and contented and rich with humour.

'Yes,' I said, 'I think so.'

My tongue was new in my mouth. The words were iron filings on the magnets of my teeth.

'You were totally out of it. Talking in your sleep.'

'What. What did I say?'

'Something about lapwings, I think. And you were shaking your wrists. You were having funny dreams, funny lady.'

I twisted to look at him. He was forty, fifty years old. He had a black beard and a white smile, and he rolled down to meet me, nose to nose, and he closed his eyes and kissed me on the lips, and in the rush of it I forgot how to use my mouth. He drew back, puzzled, and studied my face, and there were hoofbeats in my heart.

'Everything all right?'

'Yes. Yes. Fine.'

These teeth. I hauled myself to sitting, even as he laid a hand upon my shoulder. Behind him, a click, a click, a click.

'I'm sorry, Lou. I know it's boring. I hoped you'd be happy with your book.'

'I am.'

'You seem pissed off with me.'

'No. Tired, that's all. I've been asleep for years.'

He laughed at that, although I was not joking. The heat of him surprised me. It had been so long since I'd spun inside the orbit of another person.

'This'll run for another thirty, forty minutes,' he said. 'Until the light's gone. That okay with you?'

'I'm going to the shore. I want to see the sea.'

'Again? Funny lady. I'll yell when it's done.'

He touched my hand, my hip, and turned away. The clicks clicked beside him. I sat up, seeking and settling into the tidelines of my body, and studied the sound. The man had a camera on a tripod. It took a picture every few moments, every few heartbeats, a click, a click, a click. The photo showed on a tiny screen in a pulse of light, and then the camera turned to black, and then the next picture rolled about. The man balanced a computer on his knee. Two black cables spiralled into the camera. Each image blinked onto the computer screen.

He was taking countless photographs of the coast, of the few poor houses of my Sanndabhaig. He'd captured the ruined houses and the snake of the road, but hidden the masts and the fish farms in the rolling of the coast.

He tapped a button on his computer and muttered.

I stood slowly, struggling for balance, and took unsteady steps down the slope of Orasaigh towards the ocean. At every pace, rising to meet my arches, peat caressed the soles of my feet and remembered me. Heather scritched my ankles. The movements of the shore wind touched hands to my bare shoulders, saying welcome, welcome home, you're back, welcome back.

'Thank you,' I whispered. I walked. The rocks of the shore traced a song of homecoming and the sea heaved against my islands, three in a row, Dioraigh, Gasaidh, Eilean a Mhadaidh. Uist stretched away in curves and shatters, frozen in time, dropping into water. The sea churned against the rocks and murmured *we're hungry, we're hungry, feed us, come and feed us.*

'I haven't started breathing,' I said.

My body filled out and found the contours, taking the shapes that fit me best. The sea ached for me. When I reached the water of Lochcarnan, it was already sliding up the shore, chopping at the rocks and slopping, spilling salt on stone. I dangled my legs into the sea and the water washed around me and about me and poured in through the soles of my feet and sluiced out the blood until I had seawater for my heart and at last, with a whinny, I could breathe into my own true lungs. They were wet and they were dark and they were fringed with weed. My teeth curved back to fit my mouth. I felt things crunch and snap in my ankles.

'My name is Lou,' I said.

I sat there until the sky shaded into gloom and the man came to find me and take me home, saying, 'I'm finished, honey. Shall we go? I'm starving.'

Starving, said the sea. *So hungry. Feed us. Feed us. Feed us.*

'I'm ready,' I said.

We walked away from Lochcarnan, though it called for me, it ached and moaned to have me back. The sea gets so hungry. The man carried the tripod over one shoulder, everything else in a rucksack, and talked all the while about exposure, shutter, iris, light.

How could he not hear the sea? How could he be so deaf?

I spun in his wake, an eddy, tugged along and turning at the small of his back. He led the way to a campervan in the back garden of the Orsay Inn. He set the tripod down outside, ignoring spots of summer rain, and clambered inside. The computer screen was a tiny sun in the gloom of the van.

'Would you make a brew, love? I want to process this lot.'

He began to hit keys quickly. He hadn't noticed I was barefoot. My bangles were perfect circles that turned themselves around my wrists. I explored the drawers until I found a knife.

I closed the door.

'Sure you're all right, honey? You're very quiet.'

'Enjoying the silence.'

'Loudmouth Lou?' He snorted and turned back to his computer. 'That's a new one. Wait till I tell your sister.'

He fiddled with the cables, cursing as they did or didn't do whatever he wanted. At last, he broke into a smile, white teeth, white teeth. He was a small boy trapped inside a man.

'It's ready. Come and watch it through.'

I made the two steps across the van and crouched behind him, resting my chin on his shoulder. His heart pounded shudders in my neck, the warmth and the life of him seeping into my skin and it stopped my breath.

'You're freezing,' he said with a laugh, and pushed me away. 'Look.'

He tapped a button on the computer, and the screen moved – the headland came to life and moved – time poured through my Sanndabhaig, flickers in the tall grass, tumbles in the clouds, the shiver of the ocean. He'd framed the picture to show only the ruins and the road. They were the only static things, the only constants, as though they were in some way permanent, and it was the sea and sky that were flitting things, and he had turned the order of the island on its head.

Men. Centuries spin by, and still they believe themselves masters of the land they feed from.

'Dunno why they call it Sandwick Village, anyway.'

'Sanndabhaig.'

'Nothing here but stones and heather.'

'There was, once. There used to be a village. Fishermen, peat cutters, crofters with their beasts. There was seaweed, and whisky, and mussels, and song.'

'Huh. What happened to them?'

'A kelpie was born, and the kelpie ate them all.'

'A kelpie?' His face was all screwed up. 'That book of yours a fairy tale, was it?'

'No.'

He shook his head and turned back to the computer. He hit a button and the pictures flickered through again. He was in love with what he'd netted.

'I've got the best job in the world. Time-lapse captures the soul of a place.'

'Soul?' I said, only it came out a snort. 'That's a soul?'

'Yes.' He looked hurt. 'That's what I do.'

I waved a finger at the computer, the camera, the cables. 'That's not soul. There's nothing there but copies.'

'Lou?'

'You can steal them, but you can never keep them.'

'What on earth has got into you, babe?'

'You can always tell a kelpie,' I said, 'because their feet are back to front.'

A smile bloomed and died on his lips. He frowned and moved to say something, then didn't. He didn't want to look at my feet. He didn't want to, but he couldn't stop himself. His eyes were drawn down like the weight of sleep and even as his mouth fell open I put the knife into his neck. The great engine of his heart did all the rest while he clawed and scrabbled at the blade, the handle, holding in the fluid, letting it run out. He tried to push past me for the door, clutching his neck, but he was weak, and the blood made me stronger. I tipped him back onto the little seat and then brought him to lying on the floor of the van. He flapped an arm at my face but his fingers were feathers and I said, 'Hush, hush, hush.'

I took the knife and peeled back the curtains of his skin to find the staging of his ribs. Like actors slinking to the wings, I walked my fingers inside him, seeking out the private places, letting in the light.

'Lou.' He clung to the edge. 'No. No.'

'Hush, now.'

And there, at last, I found it. Between the kidneys, underneath the loops of his intestines, snugly bound about the liver – the cord that fed his soul, the umbilical that pumped him full of life. I used the knife to prise it free, to snap it out, and it came loose in a spray

of fluids. The man had stopped moving. He pooled and stiffened at
my ankles. The floor was wet and something dripped. I held the
cord in both hands and ripped the gristle with my teeth, seeking
the light. The cable began to thin and stretch and loosen and then—

> it blazed
> it slipped into my throat
> like an oyster from the rocks.

. . . and that's the soul of a place.

I walked away from Sanndabhaig.

I walked across the road and through the ferns and to the rocks
above the little harbour.

The sea was a sigh, a lover released. It had nothing else to say. It
was fed and the land was sated, for another year or two. Scratch the
surface, and you'll draw the blood. Part the web of veins, and there
you'll find the soul.

I walked into the sea. Where the waves lifted my feet, I let them
take me, let my clothes flood and wash with water, let it draw me
home, let it lull me back to sleep on my bed of bones. I found my
seat on the seabed by the cable at the foot of Sanndabhaig and lay
back against the rocks.

The cables ran from one island to another.

All cables run from one island to another.

I drifted, slipping and sliding on the tugging of the tide. As I began
to fall asleep, the bones rolled over and fell against the bones. As
the dark swept in to swaddle my dreams, they made a sound I almost
recognised, a sound I thought I knew.

A click. A click. A click.

Kenny Taylor

CULL

Sometimes there was an instant of silence before the sky exploded with noise. That's how it could seem, at least when you approached the edge of the colony. Turn a corner, stop and there they were; momentarily unaware.

Gulls, thousands of them, stippling the island's turf and rocks with the whiteness of their bodies and the grey or charcoal of their wings. Sea foam and storm clouds caught in those colours, almost monochrome, but with undertows of other tones. Close-to, the yellow of each eye a needle of sun, bright, fierce and more than a little threatening.

Then one, two, a hundred notice and react by screaming alarm as they take flight. Some others stand their ground, stiffening wings and necks and shouting defiance from the tops of boulders. I see them silhouetted, the slimness of beaks and legs, the sleekness of each body revealed against sunshine on the sea beyond, where the surface shimmers like fish scales. Silver, gold, black, grey. And white noise; the din of gull calls. 'This is our place, this is *our* place!'

And so it had been, for centuries, millennia maybe, until then. Herring gulls – those were the main gulls on the island at that time, plus some pockets of blackbacks, both great and lesser. Kittiwakes with nestfuls of gentle-looking chicks thronged the cliffs. They were roamers of the waves and deeps, able to range the North Sea over. The inland isle was the domain of the other, larger gulls. They could fly out far from land too, but their usual gliding ground was much closer inshore.

Named for the fish that had once shoaled by the billion around Scottish coasts, herring gulls had been linked to people for generations here, back at least to the time when the island got its name. '*Måke Øya*', '*Maw-aey*', '*May*'; the shift from Norse 'Gull Island' to the 'May' of recent centuries is like an exercise for jaws and lips. It speaks volumes – across the times when gulls thrived on what people threw away.

When the fishing was from small wooden boats they'd have followed (even, who knows, near a Stone Age canoe), watching as lines were hauled, quick to grab anything flung overboard. Fish heads, glistening guts, small fry, starfish; raw material for the gulls of Fife, fit to recycle into wing feathers and sinews and to keep the spark in those eyes alight.

They'd have followed the brown-sailed trawlers too; the old, broad-beamed ones, then the black-hulled Zulus, then the steam drifters with their smoking funnels and ever-bigger catches. Still the rain of debris would have come from deck to sea – the unwanted fish of no commercial value and the innards – to nourish the scavengers, the gulls most of all.

And when the herring shoals slumped and the big fishing faded, there were still some inshore boats for them to follow back to the harbours of the East Neuk, once creels had been hauled for lobsters, velvet crabs and prawns. But by now it wasn't so much the fishing that sustained the gulls of the May. It was rubbish; great, stinking, bulldozer-shunted mounds of it.

Landfill sites near the coastal towns, where the detritus of urban life was dumped and shovelled and shaped and earthed over; those were the takeaways of choice for the gulls. Some nests carried signs of the shore-based dining. Bread wrappers, packaging for bacon and fast-food meals, plastic toys from cereal packets. And the evidence of visits to raw sewage outfalls was there too, in the condoms and tampons coughed up amongst the sea pinks and green stems of the island turf.

The transformation of rubbish to gull flesh was an appealing one, I reckoned, even if I sometimes recoiled from the din, from the attack dives of angry parent gulls as I neared a nest, or the hot blatter of shit over hair and clothes. But there was a problem, said the powers that now sought to shape the island's wilds and 'manage' them according to their plans, their targets and policy statements.

Too many gulls, that was the issue. Boosted by the landfills, the sewers and some bycatch, the population had boomed. The island was becoming a gull slum, some said, with the plants suffering and other birds kept away. There was no sign of it stopping, so something would have to be done. There were census figures to show the trend, science to underpin action. And it wasn't as if the big gulls were particularly appealing to many people, in any case. Kittiwakes, with their fluffy chicks and limpid eyes, might have been different. But those other gulls, the gimlet-eyed, raucous dump-pickers, had to be reined in. A few thousand less would scarcely be noticed, after all.

So the plans were made. A cull would be carried out by a team of 'conservation' workers from the mainland, assisted by island-based staff. I was that staff, and if I was to keep my summer job, I had to comply with the campaign, to help with its execution.

*

They arrived early one morning at the jetty, a small group of anorak-clad naturalists ready to do business among the gulls. The tactics were simple – to place small squares of bread beside each nest. The bread was to be smeared in margarine. The margarine would be laced with poison. On returning to its nest, a gull would see the food, swallow it, then slowly fall asleep, eventually dying of hypo-thermia. A return from the cull team to the same part of the colony a day or so later could take out its mate.

Plastic gloves were to be worn at all times and corpses would be collected after a few hours. Any questions? I wanted to ask why, to speak up for the gulls, to say no. But I stayed silent.

Laying the bait was straightforward at first. Just locate a nest (the gulls always took flight on close approach) and place the bread beside it, perhaps a hand's-span from the cup of woven grasses where a clutch of speckled olive-brown eggs was nestled. Not many eggs had hatched yet. But where they had it didn't take long for things to turn ugly. A woman in the party was the first to find a brood. The gull chicks beside her were covered in pale down, dappled with darker spots. 'This will be useful,' she said, raising the thick stick she had been carrying to fend off low-flying parents. She brought it down with a thud on the first chick's head, then the next, then the next. Then she moved to another nest. 'Less work for future years,' she smiled.

I felt paralysed by what I'd just seen: a naturalist, a person I'd thought would have a passion for life in its mind-boggling array of forms, taking life away in such a casual fashion and seeming to relish the killing. She noticed that I was still standing in the same place; must have noticed my expression. 'It's for the good of the island, you know. We need to control these gulls or the whole place will get overrun with them. Come on, there are plenty more baits to lay!'

And I continued, plodding along with my bucket of deadly bread, following orders, watching more chicks have their skulls smashed in, noticing that the other killers didn't seem to mind either, noticing that they didn't use the word 'kill', preferring 'cull' or 'control', wondering what the hell I was doing and why I could think of nothing to say, nothing that would stop this,

*

Collection of corpses came later. A lighthouse-keeper helped by bringing a tractor-drawn trailer to different parts of the central island track, where piles of bodies could be dumped for collection. Not every gull was dead when you found it. Some still had flickers of movement in wings and feet and made strange, drunken-seeming efforts to escape.

This lack of coordination, the flailing of limbs, made the whole thing worse. The once sleek and self-confident possessors of the colony were now themselves possessed by a force which destroyed from within, stripping them of dignity as it drained away their life. A blow on the head could be a kindness in those circumstances. At least that's what I told myself, as I raised the piece of beach timber I was now using as a club, and let it fall on the heads of those who had not yet died.

But occasionally, I'd see another lighthouse-keeper, apart from the main group of people, walking slowly through the colony. Raymond had a limp, the legacy of a motorbike crash in his teens. I'd known him over a handful of years. He had a measured way with words. He'd think about things before giving an answer to a question, I'd notice, or sometimes just raise one eyebrow to make a point, non-verbally, but effectively.

Now he was moving past dead gulls, as if looking for something. Eventually, he paused and picked up a body. It flapped, feebly, but with a continuous beating of one wing. He tucked it beneath his arm and went on, moving behind a bluff of rock and out of view. Sometimes, later, I'd see him again – body swaying from side to side with the roll of his walk – as he went through another part of the colony, searching. It was near sunset when I saw him last that day, his lumpen shape in silhouette against the sea.

'They don't need to die if you can keep them warm,' he told me, days afterwards. 'Some do. But if you find a gull that hasn't quite fallen asleep, you can bring it round. Takes a few hours, but a cardboard box in the engine room seems to work for most of them.'

He saved a handful of herring gulls that way, on that day when thousands had died, coaxing them to wakefulness in warmth. He brought them back, a few at a time, snuggled them in boxes, then went out to look for more. He kept them until dark. Then he released them, lifting each to the air and letting it rise from the island to catch the updraughts from the open sea.

*

By early evening, the mounds of corpses were ready for destruction. Doused in petrol, they were torched. Feathers are quick to vanish in flame. Meat and bone take longer. An oily smoke, sometimes pale, often dark, rose above the island.

It was such a calm evening, I remember – the coastlines visible from Stonehaven to St Abbs, the sky clear of cloud, the water smooth. Only the faintest of breezes moved the air and smoke eastward, from the mouth of the firth to the wide, wide sea.

I watched until night came and the stain from the pyres blended with the dark. And the silence; the silence was unending.

Valerie Thornton

FAMILY

My mother, who is always cold,
loves her large family
of pullovers and cardigans.

She gathers them around her
and caresses their cashmere,
angora, mohair warmths.

Maybe a baby-blue round-neck
today? Tomorrow, a V in scarlet,
olive, ochre, lilac or beige?

She bathes yesterday's palest
of pink in elbow-warm water
with kind white suds

then wraps it in a fluffy towel
and presses out the drops.
She carries it to her bedroom,

arranges a cradle of netting
and, smiling, watches over
as it dries itself to sleep.

Aisha Tufail

IF

He stood at the fireplace, stroking the top of the marble mantelpiece. His eyes wandered through the soft swirls of the marble. She sat at the dining table poring over the newspaper, her eyes moving rhythmically back and forth. Then he turned towards her.

'Did you watch it last night?'

'Whit?'

'The telly.'

'Naw.'

'I did. Guess whit was oan?'

'Whit?'

'That family tree programme. *Who Do You Think You Are?* And guess who was oan it?'

She continued reading the newspaper, her head down. Then her voice floated up from her downturned face.

'Who?'

'Guess?' And as he spoke he stood facing her. Eyebrows high and a wide grin on his face.

'I don't know.'

'Billy Connolly!'

Silence. He looked at her, waiting. The uplifted corners of his grin sat down again.

'Is that no quite interestin?'

'Whit?'

'That Billy Connolly wis oan it.'

'Aye it is.'

'But y'know whit was *really* interestin?'

'No. And I don't wanna guess.'

He started walking slowly towards the dining table. Sat down next to her with his elbows on the table and leaned in and in a half whisper said, 'His great-grandfather wis in the British army in India!'

Silence.

'And . . . his great-grandmother . . . wis Indian! Billy Connolly has Indian blood in him!'

She lifted her head slowly, as if pulling against a stringy, invisible glue between her and the paper, and looked straight into his eyes.

'Really?' she asked.

'Aye, really.' He leaned back and folded his arms. Grinning.

'So like his great-grandmother wis a . . . *real* Indian?'

'Aye.'

'No a white woman born there?'

'Nope. In-dee-yun. Brown.'

'Well how d'you know she was brown?'

'Indians usually are, y'know. I mean, we're Pakistanis and we're brown. They're next door.'

'Am no,' she replied, lips pressed together.

'No whit?'

'Pakistani.'

'How come you're no?'

'I wis born here.'

'And?'

'Am . . .' and she paused. 'Am Scottish.'

'Listen, see when ye fill in all those wee boxes for yer *eth-nee-city*, do ye fill in white?'

'Naw.'

'Scottish?'

'Naw.'

'Brit-ish Pak-is-tani?'

'Aye.'

'Well then yer Pakistani. That *British* is just there to make ye feel better. And so no one like you complains. Anyway, if Pakistan hadn't been created, we would have still been called Indians. And we're brown. So she must have been too.'

Silence.

'Listen, close yer eyes a minute,' he said.

'Why?'

'Just close them. Imagine . . . Billy.'

'Fer—' she started.

'Just hold it. Close yer eyes and imagine him. Standin on stage. With his banana boots on. Now, look at his face. And just think and brown him up a bit. Y'know, a bit of foundation.' He paused and squeezed his eyes shut. 'I can see him! He looks like . . . Chacha Irshad!'

'So he does!' she cried, eyes closed.

'Wait . . . put a *shalwar kameez* on him! Can you see him?'

'Aye!'

'Now put him in a *dhothi*.' And with her mind's eye she wrapped it round him.

'I've put a white turban on his head.'

'Tie his hair up.'

'I have. He looks like a *wadera*!'

And they both sat at the dining table. Eyes squeezed shut, deep lines on their foreheads, facing each other. With an Indianed Billy floating between them.

'His long hair with his moustache. And beard. Oh my . . .'

He snapped his eyes open. His lips straight. 'He looked like a . . . the pictures of y'know . . . fighters in Afghanistan and stuff.' He sat silently, a little shaken. He flicked his eyes towards her. She had gone back to her newspaper. He cleared his throat and started again.

'I was quite shocked when I heard it. Made me think.'

'Thank God,' she whispered.

'Well . . .' and he rested his elbows on the table again and leaned towards her. 'What would Billy have been like if he was still in India?'

'Whaddya mean?'

'Well . . . what if, his great-grandmother and great-grandfather didn't come back to Britain? They stayed there. Then Billy's granny would've been there. If she'd then married into an Indian family . . . well that's it, Billy would've been Indian through and through. Billy would've been brown. And no just from the outside. The inside too.'

'Well he wouldn't've been Billy then.'

'How no?'

'Look, his grandmother did come back to Britain. She married a Scotsman. Billy grew up in Drumchapel, worked in the shipyards in Clydebank. That's why he's Billy.'

'Well . . . what about genes?'

'What about them?'

'What if . . . he's Billy because of his genes? That means he would've been just as funny, just as loud, as famous, as popular if he had been born in India.'

'Look!' she said, slamming her newspaper shut. 'If his granny had stayed in India, she would've married a man with different genes. Which would have combined to make a different mum Who would've then given birth to a different Billy.'

'But what if . . . what if . . . there was a gene that travelled through his granny to his mum to him and that was the gene that made him Billy? No matter what. I mean, d'you no hear of similarities between a great-grandfather and a great-grandchild? What if, it's a special gene that would've still travelled to him?'

'Well, would he've still been a stand-up comedian?'

'Well, he would've been funny . . . in Urdu. Or Punjabi!' And at that he slammed his hand on the table and roared with laughter. 'Can you imagine Billy swearing in Punjabi? Fabulous.' He paused to listen in his head to Billy Connolly performing a routine in Punjabi. 'Maybe Dad would've known him. Lived near him. Went to school with him.'

'Dad came here to Glasgow.'

'If Dad hadn't come here.'

'Our grandparents migrated to Pakistan *from* India. Billy would've been in India.'

'His family might have migrated too.'

'Why would they have? Only Muslims migrated to Pakistan.'

'Well, what if his ancestors had married a Muslim? And they had migrated to Pakistan? And lived in Lahore? And went to school with Dad? Then what?'

Her face was covered by her hands. She moved her hands away and her face sat in the eggcup of her palm and fingers. And looked at him.

'Then . . .' she said.

He looked at her, an eyebrow raised.

'He would've been Bilal instead of Billy.' And she smiled.

Glossary

Shalwar – a pair of light, loose, pleated trousers, usually tapering to a tight fit around the ankles, worn by people from South Asia typically with a *kameez* (shirt) (the two together being a *shalwar kameez*).

Dhothi – a garment worn by males of South Asia, consisting of a piece of material tied around the waist and extending to cover most of the legs.

Chacha – paternal uncle.

Wadera – feudal lord.

Bilal – traditional Muslim name for boys.

Jim Waite

COLLOPS O COLONSAY

Lik saft watter-fillt moths
raindraps blooter wir caur.
Ah sneck oan the wipers –

dicht dicht dicht dicht dicht

Ower fest. Ah slaw them doon.

dicht . . . dicht . . . dicht . . . dicht

A birsie wee pownie,
posturin oan tap o a knowe,
gies us a guid luik-ower.

A pictur pentit in a phone-box
cruins the Hallelujah chorus,
fower-pairt, oot o tune.

dicht . . .

Craigs lik drunken rauzors
heel ower, feet i' the faem,
no cowpin jist yet.

Tyre-dunts scart a yella straund,
whaur saund-wirms hae biggit
an umptillion fantoosh wee brochs.

dicht . . .

A gray smirr o wool
flaffs oan a barbwire fence.
Aside it, a disjaskit reid scaurf.

Oan gowf greens, gowans:
oan sheep-champit fairways,
thristles.

dicht . . .

We stap bi a dyke.
A skrinkit rabbit gaups at us,
wi een nae langer there.

Yon snell kirkyaird wind
foosts the auld stanes an
chaffs awa the names.

Naebody's aboot.

Rain's aff.
Wipers aff.
Hame.

Time tae drive, lik Jonah,
intae the aipen mou
o the Colonsay CalMac.

THE IMPEDIMENTAE O AGE

Garibaldi's villa, Isola di Caprera

Whan ma chaumer quat braithin
at twinty past sax, they stappit the cloak,
and neist day lat be the calendar.

Noo, a pikit ravel surroonds
the narra bed facin the windae
whaur ah volunteered ma last braith;
takkin the salute fae the rangs o
pink stanes and scroggy growthe
oan ma island. Garibaldi's island.

Set oot in a case, twa-three swurds,
a gun, a pictur o me, chairgin
ower a square in yon reid sark,
fechtin fur ma fowk's fredom.

Mair prominent, tho, the
impedimentae o age: wheelchairs,
a brush, a kaim,
glesses, a grey swirl o hair in a tattert box,
an orthopaedic buit an
fower pair o scruntit crutches, set in
a perjink ring, lik dancers
aboot tae stert me in
a reel ah'd feenish ere lang.

An i the gairden, a white merble statue.
Nae swurd, nae guns, nae reid sark.
Jist me. An auld man, beardit, dwaiblie,
claspin a plaidie roond his shouders,
        gaups at the sea.

Fiona Ritchie Walker

A PRAISE POEM FOR MY HUSBAND'S LOVE OF BOOKMARKING

This paper thread through pages you did or didn't read,
a life journey mapped out in books around our home.
Inside a travel guide, priced in rand,
I find your place marked
with our folded Scrabble scores,
three nights of winning, losing,
red Kalahari dust smeared in your neat tallying

and here, halfway through a finished thriller,
this dried New England leaf, still gold,
from our day in Acadia, carried back
to our cabin, pressed flat for preserving.

My scruffy notes, reminders, the quickly drawn
hearts, old cinema and long-gone airline tickets.

Folded in, beside a well-worn spine,
four stamps on airmail blue,
a fragment of your father's faded writing.
Each book checked, some to keep, this steady sifting.

Today the two of us, dark hair, fresh smiles,
appear within a Julian of Norwich prayer
that fell open without prompting.

And all shall be well. And all shall be well.
And all manner of things shall be exceedingly well.

Even in death you surprise me.

COMEUPPANCE

She's not sure he's thought it through, him giving her his
password, leaving her in the study with his history of
purchases filling up the screen, this paperless path that
zapped through server, sky each time he used the card
online, shop, phone. All she wanted was to order ink, print
posters for the choir, but now he's gone to work, left her
inkless, speechless. How did she miss the clues, the years
of cover-up, such an elaboration. Hotels and flowers,
chocolates, champagne. Shop names she knows, the
intrigue of others too dark for imaginings. This one
lingerie, she's sure, and from the jeweller's a flirty
something worth two hundred pounds that's sitting on
another's wrist or finger. No wonder there was no money
for her promised anniversary cruise. He's been in such a
careless rush that his Filofax is here, balanced on trays
marked in, out, hasn't he been busy, all the days he said
were meetings nose to tail he was sniffing, wagging,
marking an initial in the margin, adding a little star. And
here, on a birthday she's known since school, a luxury
bouquet, no message, next day delivery. She's wishing
this was a film but it's her life, her toilet she's throwing up
in, her best friend he's seeing. She cries, dries her eyes,
orders ink, life goes on. The computer ticks through click
and collect, pops up a box *give your card a friendly name*,
what is technology coming to, but now it's in her mind,
she has a plan, toys with *bastard, traitor, scum*, too
obvious and anyway, it's not the plastic that's the
deceiver, better instead to christen her card for their shared
account, leave a trail, see where it leads them. She types
eleven letters, presses save, shuts down, locks up, drives to
town. In her head a PIN, in her pocket *comeuppance*.

Roderick Watson

A RAIN POEM FOR SANDY HUTCHISON
(1943–2015)

The Tappit Hen, Dunblane

There's nae sae mony meenits i the day
that a body widna ettle tae hae
    a few meenits mair.

There's nae sae mony draps o rain
that ye wadna aye be fain tae see
    a wheen mair faa.

It's time an watter that flows on by
they droon us but keep us soomin aye
    fully i the stream.

An ilka yin maun pleiter in and jine
the spate, aa thegither, whaureer it's gaen,
an naebody gets tae stand by dry
    for iver.

But ach man, Sandy, we suld hae had
at least a pint or twa mair tae doun,
and mebbe a sang, and then a dram
    tae see ye through the door.

Sarah Whiteside

WITH THEIR BEST CLOTHES ON

He stands under the tree at the end of the garden in a silk dress. Five years old today, the dress his sister's cast-off. Behind him the party rages, birthday cake and musical statues. Children stampede from room to room. Here he is behind the tree, forehead hard against the trunk, holding his breath.

Inside the house Mum's voice calls his name and then the back door opens and music spills across the lawn. Her voice comes again, closer. He looks up. Barefoot now, she balances on the door frame, gripping it with both hands. She's wearing a dress too, a buttercup yellow one with capped sleeves and a wide skirt. She's not the sort of woman to wear this sort of dress, that's what she keeps saying and it's true: she doesn't usually dress this way. But she wanted everything to be nice and she made the dress herself, stitch by stitch. She's done everything herself. It's a lovely house, they say, a lovely garden. A lot of work, she says, but the boy can tell she likes it when they say those things.

She cranes out to look from side to side. He breathes in so she won't see him, the dress's silk bunched in both his hands. He was supposed to wear a shirt with proper buttons, jeans, and the new jacket – all of which she'd laid out on the bed for him – and at first he did, standing soldier-straight in the hallway as people ruffled his hair and called him Wee Man. They kept on coming through the door for ages: grownups in outfits; girls with their bangles, bright things in their hair; boys in lace-up shoes. Talk and laughter filled the rooms and he wanted to escape, like in that film they saw where the villain left a tap on until the tank filled with water, until the man and woman had to swim right up and breathe in a tiny space at the top – until the man thought of something that would save them.

Cheer up birthday boy, someone had said, it might never happen. He saw what he must look like then. He folded his arms and unfolded them. He ran around the house as fast as he could, right up the stairs and in and out of all the rooms. When he got back to where he started they were all still there, still smiling at him. Being a grownup is a sort of game, like being in a play, except you have to keep doing it. You have to do it all the time.

Mum comes outside now, down one step and then another. She stops. Her feet are hidden in the grass, arms hanging by her sides. She stayed up late last night to ice the cake, even though she's not the sort of woman to ice cakes. You have to make an effort, that's what she keeps saying, but the borrowed makeup only makes her face more fierce. She comes across the lawn towards him. The long spear of her eye scans back and forth. She'll find him. That's what she's like. She only wants him to be happy.

They all clapped when he blew out the candles: Happy Birthday to You. Then the grownups started to tell each other how they shouldn't really have a gin and tonic – someone bent double looking for ice, someone else standing on a chair to get the gin – and the children started playing hide and seek. Amongst the muddle of noises, the boy had gone to his sister's room and taken down the dress, stuffed it under his jacket and simply walked back through the crowd of people: out. Behind the tree he put it on, then folded the jacket, jeans and shirt and piled them neatly in the long grass. It took him several minutes to get the zip done up but he managed in the end, reaching round behind himself with both arms at once.

Mum stops now mid step. That's how he can tell she's seen him. She says his name again but quieter and with a question in it. Up close there's the textured bark, patchy white and grey. It peels back like the skin around his nails. He squeezes shut his eyes. He hopes it won't be like yesterday evening, her in the doorway of his bedroom opening her mouth to say something but nothing coming out except, finally: 'Oh, love—'

And then she'd gone downstairs and he had known to take it off, the dress. This same dress. His favourite. Luckily he hadn't done the zip up that time so it came off easily enough. Later, in his pyjamas, he crept out onto the landing to listen to the voices below. 'Obviously I don't want him thinking he's not normal,' she was saying.

Then Dad: 'You think he won't find out?'

'There's not actually anything wrong with it. You do know that.'

'It's his school I worry about,' Dad said. 'His friends.'

'He's not doing it at school though, is he. He's doing it here.'

'I'm not comfortable. I'm not comfortable with it.'

'Your comfort isn't what we're talking about,' she said.

There was a long silence then.

'Anyway,' Mum said, 'he doesn't have friends.'

Now her bare feet whisper on the grass. The boy takes a peek and the bright world comes in through flickering lashes. She says his name again. 'It's all right,' she says. She stretches out a hand towards him. He stretches out a hand too. But before their fingers meet, a noise makes her turn. Two boys and a girl from his school come shouting through the door, superstars from P3: their parents his parents' friends. The boys, he knows, are called Mungo and Milo. He doesn't know the girl's name, only that her hair is so long she can sit on it, which is the most amazing thing he's ever seen. Now, out of breath, she shakes it out behind her as she runs.

Mum holds up a hand. Seeing this, they stop. The girl puts her own two hands over her mouth. Mum does look funny, like an old-fashioned policeman directing the traffic. Mungo and Milo squint at her with identical expressions, though they aren't even brothers. They stand there all of them with their golden skin: three blonde heads shining under the sun.

'We're supposed to be playing hide and seek,' the girl says. She catches up her wonderful hair into a ponytail and allows it to fall a little at a time, until it lies around her face and body. The two boys have their arms round each other's shoulders and they rock from side to side, trying to unbalance each other.

'There's no one hiding out here,' Mum says.

'We don't care,' the girl says. 'We're bored of it anyway.'

'You are, are you? Well, go back into the house now.'

'Do we have to?'

The boys stop rocking and drop their hold on each other. Milo kicks at something in the grass. Mungo raises an arm to shield his eyes from the sun. And then he makes an odd movement: stares.

Behind the tree the boy makes a small noise in his throat, a sort of squeak. He can't help it. Mungo tugs on his friend's clothing. He points.

'It's nothing,' Mum says. 'Nothing.'

'Let's have a look at it,' Mungo says.

'Yeah,' Milo says. 'Let's have a look.'

They start to jump up and down. The girl sits on the grass and puts the soles of her feet together. She flops backwards and lifts her body from the floor, balancing on her hands and feet. 'I'm a bridge,' she says. 'I'm a crab.'

Mum puts out her arms like a great big scoop and starts to walk towards them all. 'Not now,' she says. 'You need to go back in the house now.' The boys stop jumping and stare at her. There's something in her voice. They hear it.

The girl stands up. 'Fine,' she says. She swings round and the hair flies out behind her, taking a moment to catch up. The boys scamper after in a loose-limbed darting run. When the three of them are safe inside they start to laugh. The sound of it comes out across the lawn. 'Not now,' Mungo calls and his voice goes high and bendy. 'Not now.'

The boy watches his mum's back: her watching the children go, hands on hips. After a moment her head drops forward. She turns and crosses the lawn towards him.

'You're going to need to take it off now,' she says. Her jaw tightens. 'It's not that there's anything wrong with it.'

The boy shakes his head. 'I can't,' he says.

'Love,' she says, 'you can wear it later but not now. You need to take it off now.'

The boy looks up at her. He doesn't move. She kneels down in front of him. She takes hold of his arms. 'You know I love you,' she says. 'I love everything about you, even this. There's nothing wrong with it—' She looks away towards the house and back at him. 'I only want what's best for you. I only want you to be happy—' Her fingers are digging into his arms. He wriggles and tries to pull away. Her eyes search his face. 'I don't know what to do,' she says, her voice a whisper.

'I can't undo it,' he says. 'The zip. I can't reach it.'

She breathes out then. She runs a palm across the side of his face and smoothes his eyebrow with a thumb. 'Those zip things are tricky,' she says. She ruffles his hair. 'Turn around then.'

That's when he sees them: Mungo, Milo and the girl, standing in the doorway. 'Mum,' he says. 'They came back.'

She glances towards the house. 'Oh— Shit. Shit.' She's on her feet.

'Look—' the girl shouts then. She dances up and down, in and out of the doorway. Mungo and Milo pull at each other, half hugging, half fighting: laughing. Mum starts towards the house then comes back and crouches by the boy. Other children start to gather. Grownups peer out of the kitchen window. The boy can see his dad in there, putting down his plate. Dad comes out of the door and calls across the garden: 'Emma? Em? What is it?' He takes a few steps forward and stops.

The boy gathers the pale pink material and tries to stuff it between his knees. Mum puts an arm round his shoulder. She puts her forehead against his. 'We're going to have to go out there,' she says.

He squeezes his hands into fists. Nails halfmoon his palms. 'Boys aren't meant to wear dresses,' he says.

'It's okay,' she says. 'It's going to be okay.'

Beneath his clothes he's hot and cold at once. He looks down at himself. The beautiful dress is too big for him, he sees that now. Not meant for him. A joke. Mum takes his hand and leads him out from behind the tree. Smiles hang on grownup faces. Children lean against each other and look. Everyone is quiet. He sees his sister on the terrace, grass on the toes of her best shoes, scowling. The long-haired girl stands next to her.

Mum walks the boy forward across the lawn. She shakes her yellow skirt into place and clears her throat. Dad is standing separate from the others and they reach him first. He doesn't look down at the boy. He's looking into Mum's face: 'Em . . . ?'

'Fancy dress,' Mum says. 'Isn't it great?' She says it loud enough that they will hear in the house. She twirls the boy round, laughing. 'Five years old today,' she says. She crouches down beside him and puts her arm round his shoulders. 'Thank you all so much for coming to help us celebrate. We've had a lovely time.'

The long-haired girl comes over, smelling of strawberry bootlaces and cut grass. She picks up the hem of his dress and shakes it up and down so the material balloons and flaps around his legs. 'So pretty,' she says. 'I'm trying it on next.' She runs off through the house and the two boys dart out of the crowd and go after her. Dad puts a heavy hand on the boy's head. His other hand raises the glass he holds. 'To Ellis,' he says. 'My son.'

Stiff-armed, the grownups raise their glasses in the air. Another chorus of Happy Birthday to You starts somewhere in the crowd and takes hold. The boy's sister makes an L with her thumb and forefinger – L for Ellis, L for loser – secret and quick at her hip. She walks slowly towards the house and stands at the door looking in.

The previous evening, pretending to sleep, he had heard his parents come past his door on their way to bed.

'Anyway,' his mum was saying. 'It's probably just a phase.'

'You think?'

'Hopefully.'

'I hope so too,' Dad said. 'Not for my sake but for his.'

And they had gone off down the corridor, passing comfortable phrases backward and forward between them as they might do any night, stitching their two worlds back together into one.

The song comes to an end. As people start to drift away a man steps forward from the crowd: 'I'll take a picture,' he says. Dad's hand is still on the boy's head, Mum's arm around his shoulders. 'Thanks,' she says. 'Why not?' She beckons to the boy's sister and, when Briar doesn't move, says her name low and quiet. Briar comes over then, her eyes already on the man poised with his phone. She stands on Dad's foot and holds his hand. She curves back like an acrobat, like she might leap head first out of the frame. You can already imagine the photo: how the family will look, here in their lovely garden, with their best clothes on.

BIOGRAPHIES

Patricia Ace's collections are *First Blood* (2006) and *Fabulous Beast* (2013). Her work has been published widely in magazines and anthologies, most recently in *Writing Motherhood* (Seren), *The Café Review* (Maine, USA), *Poetry News* and *Magma*. She has also been longlisted in the National Poetry Competition three times.

Juliet Antill lives on the Isle of Mull in a state of Zen mindfulness. Her poems have been seen most recently in *The North*, *Magma* (Europe issue), *Northwords Now*, *Prole* and *Snakeskin* (online). Due to a visual impairment she composes poems internally.
julietantill@yahoo.co.uk

Douglas Bruton throws words together. Sometimes they make sense and sometimes they even make stories. He has been published in *Northwords Now*, and in *Umbrellas of Edinburgh* by Freight Books, and in *Landfall*, an anthology of new writing from the Federation of Writers (Scotland).

Becky Carnaffin was shortlisted for the Bristol Short Story Prize in 2016 and was a participant in Edinburgh City of Literature's Story Shop at the Edinburgh International Book Festival in 2017.
@beckycarnaffin

Jim Carruth is current poet laureate of Glasgow. He is the founder and current chair of St Mungo's Mirrorball, the Glasgow network of poets. His most recent collection, *Black Cart*, the first part of the Auchensale Trilogy, came out in 2017.

Lynn Davidson is a New Zealand writer living in Edinburgh. She writes poetry, essays and fiction. In 2016 Lynn was the recipient of a Bothy Project Residency and in 2013 she had a writing fellowship at Hawthornden Castle. 'Leaving Bass Rock Gannet Colony' is from her collection *Islander* which will be published by Shearsman Books in 2019.

Beth Frieden is an actor and poet from New Hampshire in the USA. She learned Gaelic at Sabhal Mòr Ostaig and speaks it at home with her partner.

Harry Josephine Giles is from Orkney and lives in Edinburgh. Their latest book is *Tonguit*, shortlisted for 2016's Forward Prize for Best First Collection, available from Stewed Rhubarb. They are studying for a PhD at Stirling, co-direct the performance producer ANATOMY, and have toured theatre across Europe and Leith. **www.harrygiles.org**

Rody Gorman was born in Dublin in 1960 and now lives in Skye. He has worked as writing fellow at Sabhal Mòr Ostaig, University College Cork, and the University of Manitoba, and is editor of the annual Irish and Scottish Gaelic poetry anthology *An Guth*. He is a practising poet with a number of publications to his credit.

Brian Hamill lives in Partick. He has been an editor at *thi wurd* books for five years, and has had fiction published in the *Edinburgh Review* and other places. Brian spent much of 2017 redesigning *thi wurd* website, and aims to explore more possibilities for publishing writing online this year.

Lars Horn is a writer, mixed-media artist, and translator.

Sandra Ireland's debut novel *Beneath the Skin* (Polygon) was shortlisted for a Saltire Literary Award in 2017. Her second, *Bone Deep*, is a modern Gothic tale of sibling rivalry, inspired by a border ballad. She is secretary of Angus Writers' Circle and co-founder of Chasing Time Writing Retreats. **sandrairelandauthor.com**

Vicki Jarrett is a novelist and short story writer from Edinburgh. Her first novel, *Nothing is Heavy*, was published in 2012 and a short story collection, *The Way Out*, in 2015. More information at **www.vickijarrett.com**.

Russell Jones is an Edinburgh-based writer and editor. He has published five collections of poetry and edited two poetry anthologies. **www.WriterRussellJones.blogspot.com**

Now living in East Lothian, **Jeff Kemp** was raised on the other side of the world. His interest in poetry has grown, in part, as a way of processing the various landscapes – island, highland, desert, urban – that he has successively lived through.

Marcas Mac an Tuairneir writes poetry, prose, drama and literary criticism in Gaelic and English. He has published *Deò* (Grace Note, 2013) and *Lus na Tùise* (Bradan, 2016) as well as *beul-fo-bhonn / heelster-gowdie* (Tapsalteerie, 2017) co-authored with Stuart A. Paterson. He has been shortlisted for the Wigtown Gaelic Poetry Prize three times, winning outright in 2017.

Chaidh *Gu Leòr*, le **Pàdraig MacAoidh**, fhoillseachadh le Acair ann an 2015; tha e cuideachd na cho-dheasaiche air *An Leabhar Liath* (Luath, 2015). (*Gu Leòr*, by Peter Mackay, was published by Acair in 2015; he is also co-editor of *An Leabhar Liath* (Luath, 2015).)

Eilidh McCabe is a Scottish Book Trust New Writers Award 2018 awardee and has been shortlisted for short story prizes by *Mslexia*, theshortstory.net, and Glasgow University. She is the short fiction editor for the *Glasgow Review of Books*. She holds an MLitt in Creative Writing from Glasgow University.

Al McClimens is a 2017 graduate of the Sheffield Hallam University MA Writing programme. He appears regularly at local festivals and open mic events in South Yorks. Of his pamphlet, *Keats on the Moon* (2017, Mews Press), Neil Armstrong said, 'This is one small step for man, a giant leap for mankind'.

Hebridean **Kevin MacNeil** is an award-winning novelist, screenwriter, poet, editor and playwright. In 2017 he travelled through Argentina as part of the Outriders project – a visit that partly inspired this story. MacNeil's books include *Robert Louis Stevenson: An Anthology Selected by Jorge Luis Borges and Adolfo Bioy Casares*, *The Diary of Archie the Alpaca* and *The Brilliant & Forever*.

Kirsten MacQuarrie is a writer and artist who lives in Glasgow. Her work has been published by Glasgow Women's Library, YWCA Scotland, the Scottish Poetry Library and in *The Rooftop Busker*, volume 33 of *New Writing Scotland*. She is currently writing her first novel and documents her progress (or lack thereof!) in her 'Diary of a Novel' blog on **www.glasgowgallerina.com**.

Iain MacRath was brought up in Harris. His first play, *Fantom*, was performed at the Citizens Theatre (2014). He received the Playwrights' Studio New Writers award 2015. Stage adaptation *Briseadh na Cloiche* screened at festivals in Glasgow, Stornoway and Sardinia before being broadcast on BBC Alba (2018). *Taigh Sheonachain* won the Donald Meek award 2017. His poetry has appeared in *Poet's Republic*.

Ian Madden's short fiction has appeared in the *Edinburgh Review*, *The London Magazine*, *Stand* and *Wasafiri*, and has been broadcast on BBC Radio 4.

Susie Maguire is author of story collections *The Short Hello* and *Furthermore*, and editor of four anthologies, including *Little Black Dress*. Over thirty of her stories have been broadcast on BBC Radio. She tutors for Moniack Mhor and The Story House Ireland, and runs workshops. She haunts the aether as **@wrathofgod**.

Susan Mansfield is a writer and journalist. She is a graduate of the Clydebuilt Mentorship Programme and the poetry classes of Donny O'Rourke. Her work has been recognised by the Inspired? Get Writing! awards run by National Galleries of Scotland, the William Soutar Prize and by StAnza Poetry Festival. Her alternative Passion

Play, *On The Edge*, was performed in Edinburgh at Easter 2015. She
is an art critic for *The Scotsman*.

Lynsey May lives, loves and writes in Edinburgh. Her short fiction
has been published in various journals and anthologies, including
The Stinging Fly, *Gutter* and *Banshee*. She's never far from a cup of
coffee and her bag is always too heavy.

Donald S. Murray is from Ness in Lewis and now a full-time writer
living in Shetland. His latest book is *The Dark Stuff – Stories from
the Peatlands* (Bloomsbury).

Julie Rea won the Scottish Book Trust Next Chapter Award 2017
and was shortlisted for Moniack Mhor's Emerging Writer Award
2018 and a Cove Park Writer Residency. Her fiction has been
published in several literary journals, including *From Glasgow To
Saturn*, *Chicago Literati*, *Jellyfish Review* and *Razur Cuts*, and she is
currently being mentored by Janice Galloway.

Margaret Ries has had several short stories published. Her first
novel, *Shadow Jumping*, was a finalist for the Dundee International
Book Prize in 2016 and her second was longlisted for the *Mslexia*
Novel Competition in 2015. No takers for either yet, unfortunately.
She currently lives in Edinburgh with her husband, daughter and dog.

Mark Russell's publications include *Spearmint & Rescue* (Pindrop),
Shopping for Punks (Hesterglock), א *(the book of moose)* (Kattywompus),
and ا *(the book of seals)* (Red Ceilings). His poetry has appeared in
Shearsman, *The Scores*, *Blackbox Manifold*, *The Interpreter's House*,
Butcher's Dog and elsewhere.

J. David Simons' novels include his *Glasgow to Galilee* trilogy, *An
Exquisite Sense of What is Beautiful* and *A Woman of Integrity*. His
work has been shortlisted for the McKitterick Prize and he is a past
recipient of a Robert Louis Stevenson Fellowship.

Mark Ryan Smith lives in Shetland.

C. A. Steed is a writer and teacher of English living in Glasgow. Her short stories and creative non-fiction have been published in *Causeway/Cabhsair*, *Kairos*, and by the Hold My Purse Project. Find her on Twitter (ranting about politics or retweeting pictures of dogs) at @ZaciDeets.

Margaret Stewart lives in Edinburgh where she works as a research scientist. She is working on her first book, a crime novel set in the far north of Scotland. 'Orion's Mouth' is her first published short story.

Simon Sylvester is a teacher and filmmaker. Raised in Scotland, he now lives in Cumbria with his family. His short stories have been published in a host of magazines, journals and anthologies, and his first novel, *The Visitors*, won the *Guardian* Not The Booker prize.

Kenny Taylor lives on the Black Isle and edits the literary magazine *Northwords Now*. Author of several non-fiction books, one shortlisted for an international prize, he is incurably fascinated by islands, seabirds and auroras. All of these have featured in his printed and broadcast work for the BBC and *National Geographic*.

Valerie Thornton has two poetry collections, *Catacoustics* and *If Only Coll Were Two Floors Down* (Mariscat Press). She's published poems and stories since the 1980s and worked with the Royal Literary Fund since 2001. In 2012, she was awarded an Honorary Fellowship of ASLS for her writing and educational work.

Samuel Tongue's first pamphlet, *Hauling-Out*, is with Eyewear (2016); his second, *stitch*, is forthcoming with Tapsalteerie (2018). He held the Callan Gordon Award as part of the 2013 Scottish Book Trust's New Writers Awards and is featured in *Best British and Irish Poets 2016* (Eyewear, 2016). Samuel is also poetry editor at *The Glasgow Review of Books*.

Aisha Tufail was born in 1978 in Glasgow and has lived in Glasgow and Islamabad, Pakistan. She is married with three children and currently resides in Glasgow.

Jim Waite taught English in Edinburgh and Campbeltown before becoming headteacher of Perth Academy. Since he retired, his writing has been published, performed and broadcast. He has won the James McCash Prize, the Neil Gunn Prize, and the Wigtown Book Festival Scots Poetry Prize (twice). He lives in Perth.

Fiona Ritchie Walker divides her time between north-east England and her hometown of Montrose. She was a full-time carer for her husband until he died in 2016. Her poetry sequence *After Diagnosis* was published by Hybrid Press's House of Three last year. **www.fionaritchiewalker.com**

Roderick Watson lives in Stirling where he worked at the university as a lecturer, critic and writer for many years. His poetry has been widely anthologised and published in three main collections, *Trio* (New York, 1971), *True History on the Walls* (Edinburgh: Macdonald, 1977) and *Into the Blue Wavelengths* (Edinburgh: Luath, 2004).

Sarah Whiteside's stories have previously appeared in *Northwords Now*, *New Writing Scotland 34* and *POTB*, with a further forthcoming in *Riggwelter*. She has an MLitt in creative writing from St Andrews and teaches cello and piano in Edinburgh, where she lives by the sea with her partner and son.